Here's what other readers ~~are saying~~ **Howard R. Wolf and his work:**

"Meticulous work with language." – Professor Jaroslav Kusnir, Presov University, Slovakia.

"A wonderful writer: observant, sensitive, prescient, funny." – Dr. Helena K. Finn, US Foreign Service.

"An intellectual who has spent a major portion of his life grappling with the mysterious working of the human heart." – Professor Manju Jaidka, Panjab University, India.

What other writers are saying about Chris Helvey:

"Helvey's fluid writing will enthrall the reader with tight dialogue, lively characters, and descriptive images." – Michael Embry, author of the *John Ross Boomer Lit Series*.

"Count me as a believer in Helvey's talent." – Matt Ryan, author of *Read This Or You're Dead To Me*.

"Writing with his unique American voice, Chris Helvey delivers a real winner." – t. kilgore splake, author of *splake fishing in america*.

"Storytelling in a most pure form. Honest and sharp as winter wind." – Sheldon Lee Compton, author of *The Same Terrible Storm*.

Echoes

Of Loss

And Belonging

Echoes

Of Loss

And Belonging

A Duet of Novellas

Chris Helvey

Howard R. Wolf

෨   ෨

Trajectory Press, Frankfort, Kentucky, USA

ISBN 978-1-7337936-3-6

First Edition

This is a work of fiction. Names, characters, places and incidents
either are the product of the authors' imagination, or are used fic-
titiously. Any resemblance to actual events or locales or persons,
living or dead, is entirely coincidental.

Printed in the United States of America

For the children of troubled lands everywhere.

PREFACE

Creative writing is a form of dialogue. The ancient Greeks understood this. It may be that the letter and "personal" email best express this essential need for writers to transform solitude into conversation.

As a rule, even when published, a writer doesn't know who may have read one's words and what such a person may have made of them. It's generally speaking verbal bungee jumping into the void.

Echoes Of Loss And Belonging represents something special: two writers who responded to the other's work and found that each was a kind of echo of the other – not the same sound, but an added timbre that made, in this case, the two novellas harmonize as a kind of duet.

Our main characters: Chris Helvey's Earl Turner, my Ludwig Fried – may come from different American social-economic worlds, but they have common needs. One Christian and rural, the other Jewish and urban, their inner struggles are ecumenical and universal.

If they could meet, they would be able to help one another understand each other. The reader can supply the words that they cannot speak.

Howard R. Wolf, Amherst (Buffalo), NY

INTRODUCTION

I freely admit that when Howard R. Wolf first reached out to me about the possibility of the two of us joining forces on a book I was surprised and skeptical. I mean, why would a widely published, two-time Fulbright Scholar who had degrees from Amherst and Columbia, not to mention a doctorate from the University of Michigan, want to join forces on a book with the editor of a small literary journal in the Bluegrass region of Kentucky whom he had never laid eyes on?

Sure, I had a few publishing credits in my back pocket (novels, short stories, even a fistful of poems), but I'd never been published by one of the big houses, I'd never been on anybody's best seller list, and I certainly hadn't been voted as one of America's Top 10 young literary talents. Why Howard thought a book with a novella from each of us would be a good idea was a mystery to me.

However, as Howard talked about the need to share our voices, and the dearth of really good novellas (which I hope you will end up thinking *Of Two Lives On The Lower Golan* and *Behind The 8 Ball* are), and how our unique literary voices could form a pleasing duet of words on the pages, and how a pair of novellas by two distinctly unique writers might well turn out to be a very fine book, I gradually warmed to the idea.

I'm very glad I did. Working with Howard has been both enjoyable and inspirational. Over the course of bringing this book to reality, his emails (as we've worked on possible ti-tles, cover designs, editing, and how to organize *Echoes*) have been entertaining, informative, and tender. Although hundreds of geographical miles apart and formed by dramat-ically different childhoods and lives, we have found ourselves comfortably striding step for step down this liter-ary trail less taken. Granted, we're an oddly matched pair of writers (to keep the image literary, think Philip Roth meets Larry Brown), yet, I feel, a pair whose works harmonize to create what I think, and hope you agree, is an enjoyable jour-ney shared by two very different American men. Two men, one Jewish and erudite and one Protestant and earthy, who both hear the echoes of losses they have experienced and who both inwardly long for a sense of belonging, and a sense of finding their own place in a world that often seems some-how ever so slightly out of focus to them.

You may find it of interest to note that these novellas were written by two different writers in two different parts of America. They were written at separate times and originally intended to be stand-alone works by each of the writers. However, as Howard and I crossed paths and discovered each other's work, Howard recognized the potential synergy of combining the two novellas into one volume – that is in this case the sum being greater than the parts.

I think this final version of *Echoes of Loss and Belonging* bears out the truth of Howard's vision and I feel blessed to have been a part of such a splendid literary venture. I am so glad you are joining Ludwig and Earl on their journey. I hope you enjoy the trip. I'm sure you won't forget it.

Chris Helvey, Frankfort, KY

Contents

Behind The Eight Ball

Chris Helvey

Chapter 1

EARL TURNER turned left onto the old Johnsonville Road, rolled by Tyson's General Store, where only the security light by the pumps burned, crossed the C&O tracks, slid by the Freewill Baptist Church, then eased onto the broken asphalt that circled around Grider School, well, what was left of it. Nobody had gone to school there since all the schools in Hickman County consolidated twenty years before. For a few years they'd tried to use the building for community meetings and a place to vote. After that, vandals and critters had moved in.

Beams from the headlights reflected off broken glass in the windows and revealed the front door standing ajar. Eyes glittered from the steps. Coon or possum, Earl figured as he swung the Charger behind the building and came out on the side road where they had parked the buses. A line of burr oaks grew here and the canopy hung thick and low and the shadows were as dark as dried blood.

Earl braked to a stop and shifted into park. Then he cut

the lights and turned the radio volume down so that the dispatcher's words were nothing more than the chatter you heard sometimes on a landline when a relay switch failed and the circuits remained opened.

He hadn't gone to school at Grider, but he'd played ball in the old gym, and he'd dated a couple of girls who'd gone to Grider. Had even gone to a prom there one night. That hadn't been overly pleasant. Being a boy from Dorton, he hadn't been particularly welcome. But Rosemary Clevenger had been a sweet girl with about the nicest smile he'd ever seen. Earl scratched his head and wondered where she'd ended up. Last he'd heard she'd been working for some radio station down in Biloxi.

He'd never figured it out, but there was something about running radar at night at Grider that made him power the windows down. Usually he kept them up and the AC cranked, but it was different at Grider.

He pressed the button and felt the flow of the warm, moist August air, spiced with the scents of Boyd Braxton's barnyard, fresh cut hay, and mimosas blooming. Earl reckoned that mimosas blooming were about his favorite smell in the world. The scent signified summer for him and reminded him of when he was young and had more of his hair and less of his gut and had scored 26 one night in the District finals against Grider. Earl rubbed his paunch, then reached for his coffee.

Coffee was something he needed these days to stay awake. Only he had to take it half-caff or he'd be fighting the urge to piss all night, a fact that made Earl mad. All the getting old shit was supposed to be for retired farts, and he was barely past forty.

He eased the lid off his coffee and sipped carefully. Damn McDonald's brewed their coffee so hot it would burn a man's lip ten minutes after he bought a cup if he didn't watch it. Earl still remembered when that stupid blonde over to Poindexter had dumped a full cup on him when he was going through the drive-thru. He'd cussed her till a fly wouldn't light on her and she was lucky as hell he hadn't arrested her ass. Even now, five years later, if he ever pulled her over she could count on a ticket for everything he could think of. Denise had been her name. Skinny, stupid, blonde slut. Made his blood pressure jump just remembering how freaking hot that coffee had been.

At least a man could still get a good stiff cup of hot coffee. So many other things seemed to have changed beyond recognition or disappeared forever. Like the days when blacks and Mexicans knew their place, and women stayed home to take care of the house and kids, when gas wasn't way the hell over three dollars a gallon, and half the damn county wasn't on Oxy or Meth.

Hell, even the people weren't the same anymore – not even people he'd known all his life. Guys who used to be football stars now sported guts that made them look like they'd swallowed a watermelon and all the cheerleaders from back in the day sagged in all the wrong places. Earl sipped his coffee and tried to figure out where the train had jumped the tracks.

The throb of a motor caught Earl's attention and he looked up in time to see a farm truck rattle by. There was always some reason for pulling a vehicle over: taillight out, expired tags, a touch of erratic driving, but Earl didn't feel like pulling the truck over. Probably some old farmer rolling home after supper at one of the diners in town. Earl took another sip of coffee. He was on pace to make his ticket quota for the month and, besides, farmers were local and tended to have friends. He'd save his energy for something with more potential.

His left leg was starting to stiffen, so he popped the door and swung his boots onto the gravel. A month ago, running after some kids who'd been smashing car windows on Cedar Street, he'd twisted something behind his knee. Earl sighed. He was getting too old for that running shit.

Earl fingered his gut. Too old and too fat. Simply eating too damn much, especially late at night. Then staying up till daylight watching old black and white movies on Channel 11, or poking around on the computer and then sleeping in till it was too late to get in a good workout before his next shift. Grunting a little, he pushed off the seat and stood.

For a moment he lingered beside the patrol car, listening to the sounds of the night, not sure what he was going to do. Then he took another hit of coffee and started walking.

He didn't have a plan; he was merely stretching his legs. Shadows under the burr oaks were thick and dark, reminding him of pools of deep water and he stepped deeper into them, like he was wading into Braxton Creek. He hadn't been swimming for a long time, nor fishing either. Where in the hell did his days go?

It hacked him off to not get more done than he did. Coach Weaver had always stressed the accomplishments in a man's life. Well, he sure didn't have much to show for better than forty years on Mother Earth: no wife, no kids, and after six years on the force he was still a lousy patrolman pulling the graveyard shift.

Now the shift was his choice. Still, he hadn't amounted to much. He didn't belong to clubs or a church and he sure as hell didn't make speeches about drugs to school kids. He'd given up hunting and fishing a few years ago and never had taken up golf or tennis.

What a life – it pissed him off. Only not enough to do

anything about it. At least he was honest enough to admit that. Sometimes it seemed there was a giant sinkhole in his life and the days just kept sliding down into the hole, into the darkness. Earl could feel a pressure on his bladder and he stepped deeper into the darkness, unzipped, and took a piss. As he pissed, Earl sipped on his coffee. He supposed that was at least one accomplishment – he could drink coffee and piss at the same time.

When he'd finished, he zipped up and started back to the car. He'd have preferred to walk around behind the old school. The gym was back there and he wondered if there were any memories wandering around in the dark. But he hadn't radioed in and it would be just his luck for hell to break loose while he was away from his vehicle.

Halfway to the cruiser he heard something. It wasn't much – merely a squeak that didn't belong. That was one thing being a cop did for you – taught you to hear the things that didn't normally belong. Staying alive as a cop meant that a man had to use all his senses all the time. Had to hear the whispers and see the shadows, feel the faintest breath of air, smell the fading trace of perfume. Plenty of bad asses and dumbasses were out there. Anyone of them could kill you.

So he stopped dead still and started breathing real shallow, listening intently. In the first few seconds there was only the faint ventilator sound of his own breathing. Then, the whisper of wind up high in the burr oaks and the whine of a mosquito, mingling with the barking of a dog at some distant farmhouse.

Earl could feel the press of cooler air against the side of his face and a trickle of sweat down his ribcage. He could feel the soft thumping of his heart and the echoing throb of pulse in his temples. The taste of coffee, adulterated with a hint of fear, was in his mouth. The fingers of his right hand closed more tightly around the butt of his revolver.

Then the sound came to him again. Another squeak, louder this time. Off to his right, deeper in the shadows, somewhere behind an old school bus the county had lost track of. Earl bent and eased his coffee cup to the cracked asphalt. The squeak came again, accompanied by a murmuring of voices too faint for words to form, and he rose, turned, and started toward the sounds, drawing his weapon as he moved.

For a big man, Earl could move real quiet. He told himself that was the Choctaw line of his ancestry coming out. He told himself he needed to start passing on seconds and skipping the rhubarb pie topped with a double scoop of Drake's vanilla bean ice cream. He told himself he could get back in basketball shape. He told himself he could make sergeant, maybe even lieutenant. He told himself he could get a woman and start living the good life, whatever the hell that was. Earl told himself a lot, and deep down he knew to the ounce how much truth there was in it.

He moved slowly, pausing once to listen, then moving on, feeling the broken asphalt beneath his feet turn to gravel and then to dirt, packed hard and grooved by wheels of heavy vehicles over the years.

Here, in the deeper darkness, the night seemed to be a different world, one alive with mosquitos whining against his ears, fireflies flickering on and off amid furtive rustlings in the dark as small creatures hurried through the lank grasses that grew almost to his knees. A bird sang out there in the dark, sending forth a high, clear, liquid note that seemed beautiful to Earl, yet also lonely. So lonely it made his eyes smart.

He could hear the voices now – a boy's and a girl's. They

were coming from his right, behind the old concrete block incinerator where janitors had burned trash for fifty years before the damn EPA got all hinky and made the schools ban burning. Even though he worked for an arm of the government, there were days when Earl wondered if no government was the way to go.

Looking somewhat like a deformed dinosaur, a dark bulk loomed up out of the dark. The moon was only a promise this night, but enough starlight dappled the ground for him to tell it was a Chevy. He tugged the flashlight out of its holster and eased closer.

Ten feet away he stopped and flicked the switch.

Heads popped up like prairie dogs and a girl screamed as she struggled to cover her breasts. Earl grunted and shuffled closer, playing the light across faces and naked flesh. Just some kids out necking. No big deal. He'd done it a few times himself. Still, duty was duty. Earl flicked the light across their faces. They were spotted with sweat and twisted into expressions like you saw on the faces of Nips in the old Godzilla movies.

"What the hell you all think you're doing?"

"Uh, nothing. We ain't doing nothing."

"Is that right? Sure looked like you were doing something to me." Earl angled the light downward. "Who are you anyway?"

"Uh, uh," the boy stammered, "I'm Bobby."

"Bobby who?"

The kid licked his lips. "Uh, Bobby Sinclair."

Earl leaned in through the open window and peered at the kid's face. He'd seen the kid before, only he couldn't remember where. "You look familiar, kid. I ever give you a ticket?"

"Uh, no sir."

The kid was sweating bullets and his hands were trembling. Earl would have bet twenty dollars the palms were wet. He shone the light in the kid's face and the boy twisted his head away.

Something in the turning profile prodded Earl's memory. "You Eddie Sinclair's kid?"

"Uh, yes sir, he's my dad."

Earl flicked the light at the girl. Her eyes were shut and her face was clenched up as tight as a fist. "And who's this, your sister?"

The boy made a funny sound deep in his throat. "Uh, yeah, sure."

Earl's nose twitched. The car was full of funky smells. If he'd gone to college he could have written a paper on those smells. He could smell the yeasty scent of stale beer and the acrid aroma of fresh sweat. The girl was wearing cheap perfume and the flowery fragrance was almost overwhelming. Someone had smoked cigarettes in the car and eaten hamburger. A dozen other scents drifted through the air: dust and lotion and motor oil, plus others so faint that only traces lingered. Yeah, he could have written a paper. Been an A for sure. He should have gone to college. Yeah, right.

The girl started to sniffle and the sound grated on Earl's nerves. He hated a sniffler. Snifflers got on his nerves, but so did the girl's tits. He hadn't seen a woman's tits in months, at least not live and in the flesh – and some nice flesh it was, too. It pissed him off, letting the girl's tits work on him like that. Hell, he was on duty, not to mention old enough to be her father. "Well, tell your sister to cover up her tits and then you two get the hell out of here."

He fixed his eyes on the boy's. The lousy punk wanted to cry, but he was hanging on to some shred of dignity. Eddie Sinclair's boy. They'd played ball against each other a dozen times. Sinclair had been a good shot. Especially if you gave him a second to get set. Well, well, well.

Earl grinned at the boy; only it wasn't a just for fun grin. "And if I ever see you back out here again I'll haul both your asses in for indecent exposure, lewd behavior, disturbing the peace, and any damn thing else I can think of." He smacked the hood of the car hard with the palms of his hands and the girl made a small yelping sound. She sounded like a scared dog.

"Now git," Earl said and gave the door a good kick. He stepped back from the vehicle. The boy twisted the key and the motor spun once, caught, then fired to life. The boy shifted into drive and the wheels sent gravel sailing. The kid didn't look up as he rolled by, but the girl did and Earl caught a glimpse of her tear-stained face in the cone of light from his flashlight. Well, that was her hard luck. Besides, crying never did one damn bit of good.

Tears, faith, prayer, all of them supposed to move mountains, or something like that. At least that's what it said in the Bible. Well, like so much else in the Good Book it was bullshit. Not that he was saying it was all illusion. For damn sure none of the dumbasses he knew could create anything positive, let alone the earth and the moon and the stars and all the plants and animals, not to mention anything close to as complicated as a human being. Earl wasn't exactly sure about God, but no man, or group of men, had ever created earth.

What he was sure about was that he wished he was somewhere else right now. Or maybe that he was someone else. North of forty, packing twenty extra pounds, working the graveyard shift at a job with no real future, and still living at home was a helluva position to be in. Lousy is what it was. Earl gnawed on his lower lip and watched the Chevy's red taillights disappear into the dark, half wishing he was behind the wheel, driving off into the night, no particular place he had to be and no deadline for being there.

When the taillights disappeared, Earl turned and started walking back to his cruiser. Mosquitoes whined in his ears and fireflies danced before his eyes while bullfrogs called from the shallow creek. Just at the edge of his mind, wisps of memories shimmered like moonlit fog.

Chapter 2

THE CRACKLE of the radio brought him out of a shallow sleep. He rubbed at his eyes and wished he had a bottle of water. His throat felt thick, full of scum. Who knew what sort of bacteria lurked in there? A man could worry if he let himself.

"Earl, you out there? You got your ears on?"

"Yeah, I'm here." Even to him, his voice sounded scummy with sleep.

"Wasn't asleep was you?"

"No."

"Hate to disturb a man's beauty rest, and Lord knows you sure enough need it."

"Dammit, Ralph, I told you I wasn't asleep. Now what the hell did you want?"

"Nice to talk to you, too, Earl. You're such a joy to be around."

Earl blinked his eyes open and drew a deep breath. Why wouldn't people leave him alone? But, no, he had to put up with aggravation at... What time was it, anyway? He glanced at his watch. Quarter to two. Time did move on when a man snoozed.

"All right, Ralph, sorry if I snapped at ya. Now, tell me what's going on." Twin beams of light pierced the darkness. Someone was cresting the ridge at George Barker's place. Why would anyone be out in the middle of nowhere in the middle of the night unless they were up to no good.

"Hurry up, Ralph, I'm on duty and things can get interesting in a hurry."

"All right, you old grouch. I was calling you about the fish fry Saturday evening. Chief wanted me to call and remind everyone."

Earl sighed. "I'm working then."

"Yeah, I know. Chief said for you to swing by for a few anyway. Said he hasn't seen you in a coon's age." Ralph Metcalf snickered. "Lucky dog."

The lights dipped and swerved and Earl sat up straighter and fastened his seatbelt. "Gotta go, Ralph. Got somebody driving reckless. Later." He cranked the motor and clipped the mic in position. Ralph was still talking.

The car swung around the curve where the Bradford boy had been real bad hurt five years ago and rattled down the straightway, straddling the yellow line. It was an old Cadillac and for sure it was missing a muffler. Earl shifted into drive and started rolling. The headlights blazed up and he drove down a tunnel of white light.

He could feel blood whirling through his body now and goose bumps were popping up all along his arms. This night might soon be getting a whole lot more interesting. He flipped on the blue lights and fired up the siren.

Just as he reached the end of the drive the Cadillac rumbled by. Earl caught a glimpse of the driver's face through the side window and felt his lips curling upward. A middle-aged Mex, rolling solo. Looked like tonight might just be his lucky night.

For a minute he didn't think the Cadillac was going to pull over and he pushed the accelerator down. If there was a license plate he couldn't see it and the left taillight was busted. Poor bastard was really going to get it.

Like a speedballing funeral procession they rolled down the Old Johnsonville Road, past abandoned shacks and barns tilting east. They sped by the burned out hulk of McKunkle's Grocery and Ted Grissom's big field where high school seniors used to hold keg parties. Doing seventy-five they whizzed by the Mount Zion Freewill Baptist Church and through the burg called Dudley.

On the far side of Dudley, population 67, Earl pulled up within a car's length of the Caddy and the driver finally began to slow. The Dixie Café still sat on the right hand side of the road just past the crossroads and the driver eased into the parking lot. Earl pulled in behind him, slipped the cruiser into park, and cut the siren.

He popped the door and swung out. Earl kept one hand on the butt of his revolver as he crunched across the gravel parking lot. These days you never knew. His nerves were singing and his left leg kept wanting to tremble, but at least, by God, he felt alive.

By the time he made the Cadillac the driver had the window down. He was staring at the steering wheel like it had all the answers to the questions of life. At least the sucker had his hands on the wheel. Earl peered in through the back window. Best he could tell the Mex was alone. Better and better.

"Wanna step out of the car, Mister?"

The Mex swung his face around and stared at Earl. The man's eyes looked like smoky black marbles and his face

13

might have been carved out of a hunk of mahogany. He sat there as still as stone. Only his eyes blinked now and then, like a lizard's. The Mex gave Earl the creeps.

"I said step out of the car."

The Mex blinked again and Earl grabbed the door handle and jerked the door open. The Mex looked up then and started to say something, but it all sounded like gibberish to Earl and he jerked the man out, spun him around, and slammed him against the Cadillac. "What's the matter, amigo, don't you speak American?"

"Some, a little, maybe."

"Then why didn't you answer me?"

The Mexican shrugged and Earl jammed a knee into the small of the man's back. The Mex grunted and Earl tugged the handcuffs loose from his belt and jerked the man's hands down behind his back. "Just for your own safety, comprehende?"

The man nodded. Earl could smell beer on him. It mingled with the man's sweat and fear, forming a sour acrid aroma. He wondered if the fool had pissed on himself.

"Now, you got anything on you that could hurt me? Needles? A knife?" Earl gave the man's arms a hard twist. "Come on now, tell me. I know you folks are big on knives."

The man shook his head. "No, no, no knives."

Earl patted him down. Other than a thin wallet, a handful of change, and set of keys, all he found was lint and one tiny blue pill.

"Oh, mon, you are in so much trouble. Driving under the influence, open container, drugs, resisting arrest."

"I wasn't resisting nothing."

"Oh, quit your whining. I hate a whiner. You'd better come on with me. There's a nice cool jail cell with your name on it."

14

"No, no, please no jail. I don't have no drugs." The man twisted in Earl's grip and Earl gritted his teeth and pushed the Mex forward and jammed a knee against his spine. Damn Mex bastards couldn't be trusted. For a drunk he was strong. Stronger than Earl had figured. He could feel his muscles straining and he was already sucking air big time. He'd have to start working out for sure next week.

"That pill is my medicine. I have a bad heart. The doctor says so. Oh, mon, you are hurting me. You're breaking my arm."

Without warning the man mule kicked Earl in the shins and twisted like a snake, snapping at Earl's arm with his teeth.

Earl backhanded the Mex across the face and followed up with a right to the gut that left the bastard gasping for air. Earl could feel his face getting hot and he knew he was on the verge of losing it, but he didn't give a damn. Try and bite him, well he'd sure as hell take care of that. Keeping one hand on the Mexican's arms, he reached around and pulled his nightstick out of its holster and whacked the bastard across the backs of the knees. The Mex went down like a poleaxed steer.

"Resisting arrest, assaulting an officer, the charges keep adding up, dumbass." He jabbed the nightstick into the man's ribs and felt a satisfying jarring that ran up his arm all the way to the elbow. Standing there in the darkened parking lot, Earl could feel himself grinning. Grinning like a sheep eating dog, his dad would say. Well, his dad had lots of expressions.

Earl gave the Mex one more jab for good measure, then started tugging the Mex to his feet. Keeping a firm grip on the man's arms, he marched him across the parking lot.

"Time for me and you to take a little ride, Kemosabe."

"No, no, I have done nothing."

"Oh, yes, yes, you have broken so many damn laws I've lost count. You need to spend a few days in a nice cool place courtesy of the county."

"What laws have I broken? Please tell me that? I have done nothing." The man turned to look at Earl and a shaft of light from the cruiser's headlights splashed across his face. Earl could see fear there, but also anger, and something else he couldn't define. For a moment he wondered what that something else was.

"You'll find all that out when we get down to the station." Earl grabbed the back of the man's neck and bent him down. "In the back seat, partner. You and me are going to take a little ride. One, I promise you, you'll never forget. Now let's buckle you up, amigo."

"But I have done nothing. I am innocent. I have a driver's license. I have a green card." The man shifted in the seat, leaning forward, pushing his face closer to Earl's. "Please, I have a family."

"So? We've all got a family. What's your point?"

"I've got a wife and children. A little boy and a little girl. They need their father. Come on, brother, give me a break."

"I'm not your damn brother and why the hell should I give you a break? Nobody ever gave me one."

"But my kids, they need me."

"You should have thought of them before you got on the road driving and drinking."

The man twisted his neck and peered up at Earl, his face yellowish, washed out in the cruiser's interior lighting. His nose was broad and his lips were thin and puckered. A few dark hairs sprouted randomly above them. He reminded Earl of a catfish. "I only had one beer. You cannot arrest a man for that, not in the United States."

Seeing the man's face so close to his own made Earl uncomfortable. He didn't like anybody getting that close to him. He put both hands on the man's shoulders and jammed him back in the seat. "Don't tell me what I can and can't do. I'm the freaking law and you're nothing, a nobody, a lousy wetback, a…"

"I have my green card."

"You have jack shit and you're going to regret the day you crossed the border."

Earl stared into the Mex's black eyes. If there was fear there he couldn't see it. It was like looking into bottomless pools of black. Drowning pools.

Dying was one thing Earl had always been afraid of. He shivered like a wet dog and his breath caught in his throat. Then he grabbed the handcuffed man by the shoulders and shook him like he was a training dummy. The man's head whipped back and forth. Words escaped the man's lips, but Earl couldn't understand them. He hated people who came to America but then never bothered to learn the language. The strange words seemed to whirl around the cruiser like small dark birds, slashing at Earl's face, pecking at his eyes.

"It'll be thirty days in jail for you. I'll see to that for damn sure. And that's only a start. When the justice system gets through with you you'll wish you'd never even heard of the United States."

"Justice system? What justice system? If I go to jail for drinking one beer and having one pill of pain medicine in my pocket how can that be justice?"

"How can it be justice for you to come here without permission and take a job away from a real American who needs it? Huh? Answer me that."

Earl could feel a strand of saliva sliding out of one corner of his mouth and he reached up and wiped it off. Then he

17

wiped his fingers on one leg of his pants.

"What work do you do anyway? What job have you stolen from a real American?"

"I work with my brothers. We do landscaping and roofing."

"So there's more of you?"

"*Sí*, I have three brothers."

"And I bet you all have families."

The man nodded. Earl could feel his legs starting to shake and he knew he was close to losing it again. A red film seemed to shimmer in front of his eyes and his brain felt like it was on fire. Sweat rolled down his back and he felt sticky and slimy, like a snake. Yep, he felt like a snake. Damn Mexicans made him feel like a snake.

"*Sí*, we all have families. And we all work. We are all working hard."

"All you're doing is taking jobs away from good white American men."

The man shook his head. "Señor Lawson, the man who hired us, said that he couldn't get enough people to work before we came along. He said they didn't want to work so hard."

"Bullshit. Are you talking about George Lawson?"

"*Sí*."

"Lousy liberal."

"I am just telling you what he said. Why do you get so angry?"

"Angry? You think I'm getting angry. Well let me tell you something, Puncho, you ain't seen angry yet."

"Come on man, let me go. I have done nothing."

"And you ain't going to do nothing either, except go to jail where you belong. Sit in there for thirty days and see how much your precious family does for you there."

"My family will be there for me."

"Maybe, Puncho, but one thing is for damn sure, they'll be on one side of the bars and you'll be on the other."

The man in the handcuffs sighed. "My name is not Puncho. It is Manuel and I have a wife and children waiting for me. I have groceries in my car. I work hard and I spend my money in your town. So why are doing this to me?" He rattled the handcuffs.

A shaft of air as cool as Alaskan ice blew through Earl's brain and he pressed his face closer to the Mexican. He could smell the man's breath and his sweat and see his teeth, bared and white.

"Because you don't belong here. You're not one of us and I don't like you. I don't like Mexicans or blacks or chinks or ragheads or liberals or do-gooders. I don't like you and you've got no business being here. Nobody invited you and nobody wants you."

Earl wrapped the fingers of one hand around the chin of the Mexican and jerked his head up. "Do you understand me, Puncho? Nobody wants you."

The man stared at Earl with sullen black eyes. Neither man spoke. The sounds of the night slowly intruded. The wind was coming up, whispering in the leaves of the black locusts and serviceberry that lined the road. Crickets chirped and an owl hooted deep in the oaks that dotted the hill behind the café.

Earl could feel the night winding down. It was growing old and tired and he felt a certain sympathy for its passing. Way in the back of his brain he knew he was starting to wind down, too. He'd reached that point where the days ahead no longer shimmered in bright sunshine and cool breezes. Times when the smoke in his brain cleared enough to see

19

ahead the days seemed to be bathed in the late quiet of a dying afternoon. Life was passing him by and he didn't like it.
Not one damn bit. But what in hell was he supposed to do
about it?

"Bastard," Earl yelled. "Stinking Mex bastard." His voice
hammered inside his head. Something whirled in his mind
and he drew back his right hand and made a fist. He grinned
at the Mex. The Mex made his face hard and lifted his chin.

"You are the bastardo, señor."

As though from a long way off, Earl could hear himself
screaming. His mind was spinning like an old-fashioned
kids' top and his arms began moving like pistons. He felt his
fists smash into the Mexican's face. There was a roaring in
his mind, like the backwash of a jet engine, growing louder
and louder.

Earl smashed his fists into the Mexican's face again. For
a moment he saw the Mexican's face quite clearly, but suddenly it looked like his own. His fists hurt and blood ran
down between his fingers, staining his palms. His brain was
on fire and there was a great roaring in his ears. Earl raised
his head and screamed at the stars. For a long time he could
hear himself screaming.

Chapter 3

DAYLIGHT WAS slipping in through the trees and sprawling across the highway. Earl rubbed his gritty eyes as he turned onto the gravel drive that ran between two lines of walnut trees. Last year's windfalls crunched under the tires. Sunlight filtered through the leaves and dappled the hood of Earl's pickup. Before the budget shortfall he'd been allowed to take the cruiser home. It was an aggravation having to drive to town five days a week before he could start his shift, but at least he had a job. Being willing to work nights and weekends helped. However, since he rarely had anything to do, working the shifts nobody else wanted suited him fine. Earl pulled in beside his mother's Buick and cut the engine.

For a minute he sat behind the wheel, listening to the engine pinging, watching sunlight paint the eaves. Robins were already hopping across the yard, paying no attention to the Rhode Island Reds his mother kept. Earl looked for Baxter, the family dog, but he wasn't lying on the stone step outside the back door as usual. Then Earl noticed his father's Jeep was missing and he popped the door and swung his legs out.

As he strolled to the back door he rubbed his swollen knuckles. Damn, but he shown that Mex a thing or two. Good thing those people had hard heads, otherwise the bastard might have had to have been transported to the hospital over at Emmitt.

He paused, turned, and looked off toward the barn and the fields beyond, trying to see all the way to the Cauley place. Becky Cauley had lived there. Becky with her auburn hair, smoky gray eyes and band of freckles that ran across her face like dewdrops.

Damn, but he'd been crazy about that girl. But she was gone. First to State and then down the aisle with some banker from Starkville.

Damn. Damn, damn, damn.

Earl had never married and now it didn't seem likely he ever would. He'd never been able to quite decide if that was good or bad.

Earl sighed, shut up his face, turned and went up the steps and into the kitchen. Morning sunlight branded the back of his neck.

His mother was at the sink, washing up the breakfast dishes, and she turned and smiled. It was a tired looking smile. These days his mother always looked tired. Earl didn't see what she had to be tired about. Oh, she had to wash a few floors and clean the house and cook three squares a day, but that didn't seem so bad. And she wasn't that old. As he walked over to the table Earl did the math.

She'd had him young, seventeen or eighteen – he'd done the math once – but he wasn't really old. Well, guess he was north of forty, which would make her right at sixty, or maybe a bit above. But sixty wasn't exactly ancient. Then again, Aunt Ellen had passed when she was sixty-three or so, and Judge Gravitt had fallen over stone dead last year at sixty-one. Earl remembered that because the paper had made such a deal about sixty-one being his number when he played football for State and then his age when he died. Like the number was some kind of omen.

Well, Earl had played ball, too, only in high school not college, and his number had been thirty-three and that birthday had long come and gone and he was still alive and kicking ass. Earl pulled a chair out and flopped down.

"Morning, Earl," his mother said. Even her voice sounded tired. One way and another it had been a long night and Earl didn't need his mother making him feel more tired.

"Morning," he said. "Where's Dad?"

"He got up early and went fishing with Ben Cauley. Said they'd be over to Black Pond if you wanted to join them."

"Naw, had a hard night. I'm going to hit the sack."

"You want some breakfast first?" His mother dried her hands on her apron. Earl watched her brush back a strand of hair that had fallen across her face. For as long as he could remember her hair had been falling down. When he'd been a kid she'd tried to keep it up with bobby pins. Earl hadn't seen a packet of bobby pins in years and he wondered if they still made such things. For the first time he noticed there was gray in his mother's hair. He supposed she was getting old. Hell, everybody got old. Nobody got out alive.

"No thanks. I'm going to go on to bed. Get some sleep." Earl rubbed at his eyes.

"I saved you back a couple of biscuits and it won't take a minute to fry up some bacon and eggs."

Earl shook his head. "Thought Ben Cauley was bad sick. Heard last week he was in the hospital."

"He was. Fluid on the lungs. Looked real bad. Earlene thought for a while he might not make it. But the doctors are pretty good these days, and they've all kinds of new drugs and machines. Anyway, he took a turn for the better over the weekend and got out day before yesterday."

Earl rubbed the sides of his face and listened to the rustle of the stubble. He could smell the lingering breakfast aromas and his stomach growled. Still, he knew if he ate, it would take him a long time to get to sleep and he sure needed some good sleep. Lately there'd been too many dreams. Dreams so vivid he could almost swear they were real. Nightmares was more like it. And those he saw enough of during the day.

"Did Becky come in to see her dad?"

"Yes, she and Donald both came in over the weekend. They only stayed one night. I started to say something to you, but you had to work that bad wreck over to Bennetts-ville and didn't get in till way after noon. You looked so tired and then I forgot."

"Don't worry about it, Mom." Earl pushed up out the chair and stretched. "No biggie. I'm going to bed." He yawned until his jaw hurt. Then he shut his mouth and started unbuttoning his shirt.

His mother stepped across the kitchen and put one hand on his shoulder. "How was your shift, Earl? I'm getting so forgetful I forgot to ask you."

Earl looked down at his mother's hand. It was soft and freckled and lined with blue veins. He hated for her to touch him anymore. Actually, he didn't like for anyone to touch him.

"Oh," he said, "it was just another night on the job."

Chapter 4

DAYLIGHT, SOFT as a baby's hair, finger-painted his bedroom. How in the hell was a man supposed to sleep in so much light? Earl crossed the room and pulled the blinds down. He liked his blinds. You didn't see many blinds these days, not the old-fashioned roller kind anyway. Earl liked lots of old-fashioned things. Or maybe what he really liked was the way things used to be.

The room was still too light to suit him and he dug out a blanket from the closet and draped it over the blinds. Then he pulled off his boots, socks, pants, and shirt and flung himself across the bed.

For as long as he could remember he'd slept in this room. His mother said that when he'd been a baby he'd slept in a crib in their room, but he couldn't remember that. Earl had half-formulated a theory that a man remembered every event in his life and that all those memories formed a sort of hunter's stew that bubbled and gurgled away deep in the bowels of his brain.

Then, for some reason Earl never had figured out, one

memory would break away from the mixture and bubble up, all the way to the surface. Earl wondered if that was where dreams came from. In any case, he'd never remembered sleeping anywhere but this room, so those baby memories must have been buried real deep.

He rolled over and lay on his back, looking around the room. As best he could tell, nothing had changed since his high school days. His old football jersey was still thumb-tacked to one wall and on another were a pair of fading posters of baseball players who were probably in a nursing home by now. His model cars still sat on the single shelf above his dresser and his weights were still piled in one corner. He really ought to start lifting again, he told himself, knowing he wouldn't.

These days he didn't seem to do anything he didn't absolutely have to do. Work, sleep, eat, watch a little tube – that was about it. Only now he was supposed to go to this fish fry, or cookout, or whatever the hell it was at the chief's house. No telling how many people would be there. Most of them he wouldn't like. Maybe he could just make an appearance – eat some hushpuppies, drink a beer, shoot the shit with the chief for a couple of minutes – then drift away into the night. Sounded like a hell of a plan. Earl closed his eyes.

For a moment he thought he was going to be able to go to sleep. It had been weeks since he'd had a good eight hours. Even seven would be almost heaven.

But then his knuckles let him know they were still aching. He rubbed them for a minute and tried to forget the pain, but they kept throbbing. If anything, they hurt worse, so Earl rolled out of bed, slipped on his robe, and padded down the hall to the bathroom. Still sharing a bathroom with his parents seemed wrong somehow, but that was the way it was.

He rooted around in the medicine chest, found a bottle of

generic ibuprofen and shook out a couple. He washed them down with a paper cup of water, then shook out two more and swallowed them. Might as well knock the pain down good, he figured.

He could hear his mother still messing around in the kitchen and knew that as long as she was banging pots and pans he wouldn't get any sleep. So he turned and went down the hall into the living room and powered on the television. For a couple of minutes he cruised the channels, but then he chanced on an old Randolph Scott western that also featured Joel McCrea.

Earl always found something soothing about those old westerns. Watching Randolph Scott or Jimmy Stewart or Roy Rogers or Glenn Ford, anyone like that, ride down a lonesome mountain trail with massive boulders on one side and towering pines on the other seemed to calm his blood. Nothing pleased him more than to flick on the television and see some lone rider entering a Mexican village just as the dying daylight turned that special blue you only saw in movies.

It wasn't so much the gunfights, they were okay, and it sure wasn't the kissing that he liked; it was more the sense of a world in which there was right and wrong, a certain order that gave a man comfort.

The ibuprofen were beginning to work and Earl massaged his knuckles as he eased deeper in the recliner. He wondered if the Mexican in the jail would get any sleep. Probably shouldn't have hit him so hard, but that's what the wetback deserved for trying to sneak into a country that wasn't his own.

Not that America was what it used to be, not with all those liberals, environmental whackos, feminists, and blacks thinking they should be running the country. Rap music made him sick and he hadn't found a book worth reading in years. Yeah, America was going to hell in a handbasket and nobody was doing a damn thing about it.

Well, at least he was fighting the good fight. Not that he could see where it made much difference. Earl wondered how long he, and the few others out there like him, could hold back the tide. He had a real bad feeling about the future.

His mother had moved on to her bedroom. He could hear her making the bed, picking up clothes, humming to herself. The soft sounds of her small movements were soothing and Earl felt his eyes getting heavy. Randolph Scott and Joel McCrea were coming to the end of their long ride. Earl had lost the thread of the plot, but it wasn't difficult to figure the climax was at hand. McCrea and Scott were hunkered down in a depression in the earth outside a ranch house, slinging lead at two bad guys in the house and a young Warren Oates who was holed up in a barn, blasting away out of the hay loft.

His mother was singing softly now – some church hymn that Earl vaguely recognized. His legs had started to ache and he massaged them as best he could. But the massaging didn't seem to help. What were his legs aching for? He wasn't that old. Maybe he had some rare leg disease. With his luck it would be fatal.

It seemed to him like he was forever ending up behind the eight ball. Some days he felt like he ought to change his name to Eight Ball. Hell, Eight Ball could be his rap name. Earl snorted – he'd do rap when hell froze six feet thick.

Scott and McCrea did a little talking, then they hollered at the bad guys, then they got up out of the ditch. Earl could see McCrea had been shot below his ribs. For a minute it looked like the two aging cowboys were going to toss down their guns, but Earl wasn't buying that. Not those two. Not the good guys. Good guys never give up, even when the rest of the world was tumbling down among them. That much he knew for certain. He'd read his dad's Chip Hilton books.

As he watched, Scott and McCrea started walking toward the house, strolling along just like they were walking down Main Street in Cowtown, USA. He couldn't figure that move out. Then the bad guys started coming out of the house and the barn and he could see it was going to be pure, unadulterated western classic.

The gunfight in the middle of the street, well the barnyard in this case.

Only this time, instead of one bad guy against the sheriff, it was two aging western heroes against three desperados. Classic. Earl liked classic.

Without any warning, all five men started blazing away like mad. His mother was singing "When The Roll Is Called Up Yonder." Even Earl recognized that one. Bad guys were dropping left and right. Joel McCrea took another bullet. Randolph Scott was blasting away. McCrea took another one. He had to be bad hurt.

All the bad guys were down. No, that lousy Warren Oates was only wounded and as Earl watched Oates plugged poor old Joel McCrea one more time. Earl felt a touch of empathy for McCrea. It seemed like somebody was always blasting away at him, too. Even when he was hurting. Now McCrea was behind the eight ball for damn sure.

Randolph Scott finally shot Warren Oates to pieces as Joel McCrea lay dying in the dust. He and Scott were talking. Earl was glad he'd hadn't turned the volume up. He couldn't read lips, but he figured they were saying their final goodbyes. Earl hated goodbyes.

As he watched, Randolph Scott stood up tall and walked away. For a second, Joel McCrea gazed into the camera, then did a slow half-pirouette and lay on his face in the dirt, as still as death. The camera panned to blue mountains rising on the far horizon. Earl's mother started singing "Love Lifted Me."

Earl shut his eyes and tried to pretend he was riding the high country with Randolph Scott and Joel McCrea. Only every time he looked at Scott or McCrea he saw the Mexican's face. Then he saw Becky Cauley's face and her smooth white arms and her long sleek legs. Then he saw only blue mountains rising from a smooth brown desert.

Chapter 5

THE ROAD ran through a grove of pecan trees. Those trees had been there for a long time and their canopies had swollen until they touched above the center of the road. Although it wasn't quite seven o'clock, the shadows beneath the pecans were thick and dark as old blood. Earl stretched out a hand to turn on his headlights, then stopped. No need to make an entrance. Okay, so he had to make an appearance for the chief, but beyond that nobody really needed to know that he was there. He wished he hadn't traded shifts so he could come to a stupid party. If he'd been on patrol he'd had a great excuse to vamoose. Instead, he'd swallowed a double shot of Jack at the house – just to settle his nerves, climbed in his truck, and driven into town to waste a perfectly good evening.

His windows were down and he could hear the crunch of pecan hulls beneath the tires. Pecans were tasty. His mother always made a pecan pie at Thanksgiving, but the chief had way too many trees. A small army could find cover in the lane. Earl preferred a clean line of fire.

By now he could see the party. It was centered down by the pond. Multi-colored lights and streamers had been strung in the willows that grew on its banks. Somebody had rented tiki lamps and jammed them haphazardly around a handful of picnic tables. Their lights cast dancing shadows on the faces in the crowd.

Damn, Earl thought, everybody who was anybody in Denton and their brother must be here. At least he'd put on a clean shirt. Still, he wasn't in the mood to take any mouth off anybody tonight. Earl spotted a gap between a Mustang and a Buick SUV and twisted the wheel.

For a moment he simply sat behind the wheel looking at the milling people, listening to the engine ping, wishing he was somewhere else. At least there would be something to drink, and he needed a drink. Bad. Earl popped the door and slid out into the twilight.

Voices rose and fell like the humming of a gigantic hive of bees. Earl felt his throat tightening up and he swallowed a couple of times. People at a party always felt an obligation to talk. Usually it was something that didn't matter much, like the weather or how so-and-so was feeling. Politics and religion, now those were two subjects it was best to steer clear of. But there was sure to be beer tonight, and probably wine, maybe a half-pint of the good stuff in somebody's hip pocket. Might even be a bottle of shine under the seat in somebody's truck. Well, a shot would taste good and might calm his nerves. Three or four of his fellow officers were standing around a covey of coolers and Earl took a deep breath and started strolling toward them. Dew had already fallen and he could see it sparkling like ground glass where the lights from the tiki torches struck it.

"Well, look who's stumbling in."

"If it ain't old Earl, late as usual,"

"Hey Bill, Gary. That you, Ted?" The men were standing under a black gum that must have been growing when Pickett led his Virginians up that slope at Gettysburg. The shadows were as black as ink and shifting in the wind.

Somebody put an aluminum can in his hands and Earl popped the top and sniffed. Beer. Well, that was all right. He lifted the can and took a long drink. Beer wasn't his favorite beverage, but it would do, especially since it was free.

Music drifted on the wind – a song with a strong pulsing beat that made Earl think of old jungle movies. Still, he'd heard it before and, if he had his facts right, it was supposed to be what was called a dance hit. Earl didn't dance. Well, maybe a slow dance every other year. When was the last time he'd gone to a dance?

"Heard you had some trouble the other night, Earl?"

Earl lowered the can and looked at Tom Underwood. Tom had been a couple of years behind him in school, a shifty halfback who could have gone to a small college and played football. Instead, he'd done a stint in the army and then joined the Denton police force. The last couple of years he'd started to develop a pot gut. Earl thought he looked like a weed who had gone to seed.

"What kind of trouble, Tom?"

"The Mexican kind."

Earl sipped his beer. "Yeah, a little. Man had a smart mouth on him."

"When I saw him he looked pretty rough. What'd ya do to him? Run over him with the cruiser?"

"Ha, you're really funny, Tom. You ought to be in a comic strip."

"His face did look rough, Earl."

"Damn, Bill, I just got here. Haven't even got a beer down and everybody's on my ass."

"Nobody's on your ass, Earl. We just want to know what happened between you and the man that looks like he went fifteen with Ali and Frazier at the same time."

Earl shrugged and hit his beer again. "Fellow got belligerent, so I had to calm him down."

Gary Woodson laughed. Woodson was one of those people who thought every damn thing was funny; at least he seemed that way to Earl. "Calm him down. The man was damn near comatose."

"Yeah, well, he had it coming."

"What he'd do?"

Earl could feel their eyes on him and could hear the smartass attitudes in their voices. They weren't really interested in what had gone on between him and the Mex. Bastards were only poking fun at him, pretending to be his friend. Yes, they wore the same uniform, but that was it. He was different and they didn't like that. Didn't like him. Never would like him. He'd accepted that a long time ago. He'd drink this beer and make a quick circuit, speak to the chief, then drift into the darkness. By ten o'clock he should be home. Again, Earl wished he'd never come. He shouldn't have traded shifts with Deke Evans, even if Deke was a Pentecostal who never drank.

"Well?"

"Well what?"

"I asked you what the Mexican did to make you beat his face into hamburger."

Earl shrugged and hit his beer again. "It's all in my report, Gary."

"Damn you're edgy tonight."

"Gary's right, Earl. You sure are tense."

"What you need is a woman, Earl," Underwood said.

"I can fix you up with my wife's sister. She's no beauty

queen, but she cooks a mean pot roast."

Underwood punched Earl lightly on the arm. "Forget about having to work for some snatch, Earl. Just roll on over to Slabtown and get you some of that black stuff. Hear it's real juicy."

Underwood leaned in closer. His breath smelled like cat food. "Let 'em know you're a cop, Earl, and they might give it to you for free."

The three other men thought that was damn funny. Listening to them laughing, Earl felt a slow burn going up his neck.

"Fuck you, Underwood. Sideways. And the rest of you guys, too." He wheeled and started off down the slope. Over his shoulder he said "I don't need your shit."

"No Earl, you need to get laid," Underwood hollered.

Earl wondered how many people had heard that loudmouth. He hated Underwood. He hated them all. For that matter, he wasn't real damn pleased with the rest of the world.

Earl kept moving, sipping beer and drifting toward the lights nearer the pond. Faces swam up out of the murky light like fish surfacing in a muddy lake. Voices rose and fell on either side and he could hear the wind working through the tops of the willows rimming the pond. Now and then a voice spoke to him, and he mumbled something in return. Once he heard his name called, but he didn't recognize the voice so he kept walking.

Even in the pools of light it was challenging to see faces. But he figured he'd recognize the chief in a tornado. After all, he'd seen the man's bony face thousands of times. All he wanted was a quick look at it tonight and a chance to say a few words, then he'd be long gone.

But there were a hell of a lot of people at the party and he hadn't even caught a glimpse of the chief or his wife. The chief's wife wasn't much to look at, but she was nice. Her face was moon-shaped and she had a double chin, but she'd always been nice to Earl when he'd had to swing by the house to pick something up for the chief. Once she'd even given him a big piece of rhubarb pie hot out of the oven. He'd eaten it standing up. She'd put a scoop of French vanilla on it and poured him a cup of the chief's coffee. That had been just about the best thing to happen to him that year. Where the hell was the chief?

Earl had reached the pond and he stood on a bank for a moment, watching the lights dance on the water, the murmur of voices rising and falling behind him, letting the night breeze slide cool across his face. Standing there alone didn't feel half bad.

Maybe it was time for him to move out on his own. Plenty of times he'd thought about it. But living at home was cheap and he didn't have to do his own laundry and his mother almost always cooked something he liked to eat. Plus, he'd never found the right woman, one he'd want to spend a few months with, let alone the rest of his life. Of course, if he'd date a little more he might find a nice girl. A mosquito whined in his ear and Earl tossed his empty beer can into a patch of reeds, turned and slogged back up the slope.

Halfway to the truck somebody called his name and this time he recognized the voice and zigged right and ambled over. The mayor and his wife were sitting at a picnic table. A Coleman lantern on one end provided enough light for Earl to see a bottle of Blanton's next to a row of small, clear plastic cups.

"That you, Earl?"

"It's me."

"Thought it was." The mayor extended a hand and Earl

shook it.

"You'll excuse me not getting up and greeting you properly, Earl. Rheumatism is acting up tonight. You understand?

"Sure, no problem, Mayor." Earl nodded at the mayor's wife. "Ma'am."

"Sue, you know Earl Turner, don't you? You don't? Well, let me introduce you. Sue, this is Earl Turner, one of our city policemen. He's been on the force quite a while. How long have you been with us, Earl? Six years, seven?"

"Something like that."

"Pleased to meet you, Earl. Now that your face is in the light I do believe I know you. You patrol on Elm and Webster sometimes, don't you." She extended a slim hand. Earl took it in his. Hers was full of bones.

"Yea, ma'am, sometimes. I work mostly at night, though."

"Well, it's good to know our streets are safe at night."

Earl wasn't sure what to say so he just nodded and let go of Sue French's hand.

"Earl, what are you doing without a drink in your hand? Chief Evans wouldn't approve. Everyone needs a drink at a party, don't you agree? Parties are for having a good time. Everyone knows that. How do you take yours, Earl? Straight, or on the rocks?" The mayor pointed the Blanton's bottle at Earl?

"Straight will be fine."

"Good, good." The mayor poured a healthy shot. "Here you go, Earl. Appreciate all you do for the town of Denton. Want you to know that."

"I try and do my job."

"And we appreciate it. Don't think we don't."

Earl nodded and sipped his whiskey. It was good stuff,

but potent. He'd have to watch it. He still had to drive home.

Mayor French leaned forward and peered into the thickening darkness. "Sue, have you seen, Kathy?"

"She went walking with the Crawford girls. They headed toward the food."

Earl felt a hand on his arm. "Earl, you know our daughter, Kathy, don't you?"

"Seen her around, I guess."

"Well, you know she's just a tiny bit, er, well let's call her special. If you get my drift."

"I understand."

"Good, good." Mayor French patted Earl's arm. "Would you mind to go and check on her for us? Make sure she's safe and sound."

Earl took a healthy slug of whiskey. He knew the girl all right. She was trouble. A nice body, but all the synapses weren't connecting up top. Not retarded, exactly. More like a step slow. She had a bit of a reputation, too. He'd have to watch his step. Lately, Earl felt like he'd been tiptoeing on black ice.

"Sure, Mayor. I'll take a stroll around and see if I can find her. If I do, I'll tell her to come straight here."

"Good, good, that will be fine. Now let me refill your glass. Walking around can make a man thirsty, and I don't want anybody to ever be able to say Bill French let anybody go thirsty."

The mayor and his wife exploded into peals of laughter. Earl faked a smile and held out his glass. He wasn't a big drinker and he'd already had plenty. At some point in the evening he'd need to drive home. And he sure as hell didn't need to get pulled over. He felt certain he wouldn't get a ticket, but he'd never hear the end of it.

The mayor finished pouring and Earl made his goodbyes

and stepped back into the darkness, just beyond the light. He began working his way around the slope, angling in the direction of his vehicle. He kept his eyes open, sure, but he was looking primarily for the chief. If he happened to see Kathy French, so much the better. All he really wanted to do was say his thank you to the chief, then head home. At least get out of the crowd. A peaceful drive down a back road with the windows lowered and some old Hank Snow and Ernest Tubb blowing through the speakers wouldn't be half bad.

Feminine laughter rang out from a line of maples higher on the bank and he angled back toward the pond, worked his way around a couple lying on a blanket and started for his truck. He crossed over a footbridge that spanned a runoff ditch, then eased by a group of women sitting around a wooden picnic table, talking about an ice cream social the Methodists were holding the next week. He hadn't seen the chief or Kathy French, but he'd had enough.

He took a good slug of whiskey then picked up the pace. Parked cars and trucks were scattered about like cattle standing out in a field at night. He couldn't remember exactly where he'd parked, but it had been fairly close to the iris bed the chief's wife was so proud of.

"Hi, Earl."

The voice made him jump and whiskey sloshed out his glass and dampened his hand. He peered into the dark, trying to locate the woman who belonged with the voice.

"Over here, Earl."

He knew the voice now. Just his luck. "Where are you, Kathy? I can't see you."

"Oh Earl, come and find me."

"This is not funny, Kathy." Earl could feel the pulse that ran along the side of his neck pounding. He was starting to

sweat and a vein in his left temple throbbed. He forced himself to take a couple of deep breaths and tried to speak more
slowly.

"Your folks are worried about you, Kathy. Come on out
and I'll help you find them."

He stopped moving, standing as still as he could. He
could hear the wind whispering in the sassafras leaves and
the rustle of a small creature in the taller grasses off to his
right. Someone had started a bonfire and he could hear the
crackling logs and see the orange flickers. Quietly, he lifted
the glass to his lips and took a healthy sip.

Earl knew he'd had enough to drink. Really, he ought to
toss the liquor into the bushes. But he hated to waste good
liquor, and, besides, he'd been on semi-good behavior for
the last couple of weeks. He took another sip. His head was
spinning a little, but nothing he couldn't handle. Now to find
Kathy and get her home. He'd get her there if he had to drag
her.

"Kathy, this is the police. You get your ass out here.
Now."

Off to his left bushes rustled. Earl turned toward the
sound. A tall, slim girl stepped into the thin reflected fire-
light. Her blonde hair seemed to glow.

"Hi Earl." She had a little girl voice that did things to men.
At least until they got to know her better.

"Kathy," he said, "you need to go back to your mom and
dad."

"I don't want to go back there. My folks are no fun."

"Yeah, well what you want doesn't matter right now."

She stepped back and pushed at him with her arms. Her
hands fluttered like pale, wounded moths.

"I'll scream. I'll scream and I'll tell everyone you tried to
rape me." She started unbuttoning her blouse.

Damn, Earl, thought. Just what I don't need. "Quit that shit," he said. "Button yourself back up."

"No. Not unless you don't make me go back to them."

"What's wrong with your parents? They seem all right to me."

Kathy shook her head. Her hair swirled in a golden orbit around her face. "They're not. They're mean and hateful and they never let me do anything."

Earl took a step closer. While he tried to think of what to say he sipped his liquor again. "I'm sure your mom and dad are only trying to do what's best for you. When you get grown up you can make more of your own decisions."

Earl wasn't sure how he should talk to the girl. Everyone in town knew she wasn't quite right, but he never had heard exactly what was wrong with her, or how bad off she really was. Earl had seen her a few times in stores around town or walking down Elm Street like she was headed to the library. Once, he seen her going into the Rialto. If he remembered right, she'd been going in to see a Disney movie.

"Ha," the girl said, her voice loud in a night gone suddenly quiet. "How old do you think I am, Mr. Earl? I mean your Officership, sir."

A mosquito whined around Earl's face and he slapped ineffectively at it. He wasn't sure how to answer. He'd never been sure what girls really wanted to know when they asked questions.

"I don't know," he said. He didn't want to offend the girl, but he didn't want her to think he was stupid. Earl rubbed his jaw. His stubble crackled. "Eighteen, nineteen, maybe."

"Ha! You are so stupid, Earl Turner. I'm twenty-five. I'll be twenty-six next month. See, Mr. Police Officer, you're not nearly as smart as you think you are."

Earl could feel his face blushing. He tilted his head back

and took a long swallow.

"Well, that doesn't change anything, Kathy. You still need to go back to your parents." Earl hoped the goofy girl wouldn't go to screaming.

The girl stamped one foot and then took a step closer. "Can't you understand? I'm not going back there. But…"

Earl felt his stomach start to churn. Before the night was over this girl was going to be trouble, that he could see real clear. He took another drink, longer this time. Yes, the world was definitely tilting on its axis.

"But what?"

"But I will let you drive me home." The girl, or he supposed she was legally a woman, started walking. She walked right up to Earl and put her hands on his chest. She began to move them in ever widening circles.

"Hey, quit that."

"But I like doing it. Your chest feels nice, all hard and hairy."

Earl twisted away from her roving hands and she let out a little yelp and grabbed his arm, sloshing his drink. Earl could feel the liquid running down his arm. He knew it was just his imagination, but it felt like it was burning his flesh. Damn, he must already be three sheets to the wind. He'd never been able to handle his liquor. The earth was swaying ever so slightly beneath his feet and if he closed his eyes he could almost swear a heavy sea breeze was blowing.

"Now, look what you've done. I could arrest you for assaulting an officer. "

"Ha, Earl Turner, you're too drunk to arrest anyone."

"Don't count on it, little missy."

"My name is Kathy."

Earl took a deep breath, held it for a moment, then let it out. "I know what your name is. Now it's time to go home."

He drained the last of the whiskey and tossed the cup into the underbrush. The earth seemed to undulate as he grabbed the girl's left arm with his right hand. "Come on, Kathy, I'll drive you home."

For a moment she resisted, as though she had suddenly become uncertain. Then, as they started walking, she murmured something he couldn't hear. In one part of his mind, Earl knew he shouldn't be driving, He was way too loaded. At the very least he ought to take a long walk and sweat some of the alcohol out. But, in another chamber of his brain, he knew he wouldn't.

He could feel the softness of the girl's skin and smell the thick, cloying sweetness of her perfume. Earl had a funny feeling. The sort of funny feeling he often got when he was about to do something really stupid.

Chapter 6

THE TRUCK'S headlights probed the darkness, asphalt unfurling beneath their glare like a wide shiny ribbon. They were on Swanson Pike, just past what was left of Talbot's Mill, where the road ran between two low hills. The darkness seemed to press down there, thick and heavy, so that it felt to Earl it was starting to set up solid, like concrete forming.

His life had felt like that a lot lately. It was as if he were rushing into a vast overarching darkness at sixty miles an hour and there wasn't one damn thing he could do about it. Earl wondered if one night he really was going to drive off the edge of the world, or smash into the final mountain.

His mind had wandered and Earl caught sight of tree branches white in the light and cut the wheel. For a minute they were spinning gravel and sliding sideways, but then the tires caught and Earl got the back end around and they were rolling smoothly again.

"Ohhh, that was fun, Earl. Do it again."

"You're crazier than I thought, girl."

"I ain't no girl and I'm not crazy."

Earl shot her a quick glance, then swung his eyes back to the road. "You are if you like taking fool chances like that. We damn near crashed."

"You don't have to yell at me, Earl. I only thought it was exciting. Can't a girl have a little excitement in her life?"

"Sure," Earl said, "only not when I'm driving."

He shook his head. The girl was definitely more than a few degrees out of plumb. Before them the road rose and fell gently under the white eyes of the headlights. Sycamores leaned their pale trunks over the road and a raccoon peered at them from the brush that grew almost to the edge of the road. Earl figured he'd been on every road in the county, and this one looked vaguely familiar, but he couldn't recall any of the French clan living out this far.

"You sure your aunt lives out here?"

"Yes. My Aunt Martha lives just a few more miles on down this road."

"I didn't know your father had any sisters."

"Uh, well, actually Aunt Martha is my mother's sister."

The left side of Earl's jaw was itching and he scratched at it. Damn mosquitoes were extra bad this summer. "Thought your mom came from Atlanta."

Kathy giggled. "She does. Aunt Martha is only her step-sister."

"Hmm," Earl started to ask another question, but just then the road made a hard right bend and he had to concentrate on his driving. He was damn near drunk. He could tell by how freaking slow his reflexes were. No way in hell he should have had that last drink, or even the one before. Handling liquor was not his strong suit. Although he knew better, the road seemed to shimmer before him. His stomach no longer felt right. He eased off the gas and inclined his head toward the open window.

"How much farther to your aunt's place?"

"Oh, not far."

"And you're sure your dad said for you to spend the night with her?"

"What? Oh yes, that's right."

The girl scooted a few inches closer and giggled under her breath. Earl leaned more of his weight against the door. Her perfume was thick and sweet. It wasn't one he'd noticed before. It was so sweet it made him a little nauseous. But it also affected him in other ways. Ways he surely didn't need to be thinking about.

"Earl, you care if I turn the radio on?"

"Go ahead."

The girl started punching buttons and in a few seconds music filled the cab of the truck. Out of the corner of his right eye, Earl could see her leaning on the passenger door, her head half out the window, her hair blowing in the wind like waving grain. Best he could tell, she was singing along with the music, off key and a half beat late. Earl shook his head. Kathy French was nothing but an overgrown kid.

Earl whipped his eyes back to the road. He couldn't take any chances. Not with drinking and certainly not with the mayor's kid riding shotgun. He concentrated on the road and the music, trying to sober up.

He didn't recognize the tune or the singer, but he'd bet the farm that it wasn't Hank Snow. The tune was catchy, but he couldn't understand a word. Nothing was like when he was a kid. Music was different, movies were different, it was hard to get a good hamburger anymore – they all had sprouts on them or had been pulverized in some two hundred dollar blender. Hell, he'd read in the newspaper only last week that there were women umpires and guys were marrying each other. Nothing made sense these days.

Earl didn't feel like he was that old, but somehow, when he hadn't been watching, the world had changed on him, passed him by like he was an abandoned car – say the '62 Ford Galaxy his Grandpa Turner had owned.

"Earl? Earl? Earl?" The girl had one hand on his right shoulder and was shaking it like hell. He must have really zoned out. He'd have to watch it. From experience, he knew he did stupid stuff when he was drunk.

"What?" he said, his voice sounding harsh, even to him.

Earl took a deep breath, held it for a three count, then let it out. "What is it, Kathy?"

The girl giggled again. Earl hated giggling. For damn sure he would be glad when this night was over. Never again was he going to drink so much again. This time he meant it.

"I gotta pee?"

"What?"

"I gotta make water."

"Damn, Kathy, I know what pee means. Can't you hold it till you get to your aunt's?"

In the glow of light from the dash he could see the goofy girl shaking her head. She was worse than some kid.

"Earl Turner, you are nothing but an old meanie and I'm going to tell my daddy on you."

Earl groaned. All he needed was to get on the mayor's bad side. One way or another he seemed to always be getting in trouble. For sure, he didn't need to get behind the eight ball again. "All right, all right, I'll pull over," he mumbled out the side of his mouth, his eyes peering into the darkness, looking for a wide spot.

Chapter 7

MOONLIGHT SILVERED the ground, finger-painted the treetops, and highlighted the blackberry patches on the slope. Earl leaned against a black gum tree and fired up a Camel, his first of the evening. He was trying to quit, but thirty year habits were hard to break. He drew smoke into his lungs and felt tension ease in his body.

Honeysuckle was in bloom. When the wind was right he could smell it over the acrid scent of burning tobacco. An owl had started up high on the ridge and now another answered him from across the road, deep in a thicket of oaks and hickories. In the glare of the truck's headlights that thicket had looked like a paradise for squirrels. He'd have to remember the spot when November rolled around.

The wind began to die and he could hear leaves scrunching as some small animal worked its way through the night. He sucked in smoke, closed his eyes, and listened. At first, all he could hear was the humming of cicadas and then the whine of a mosquito close by his left ear. After a bit he could hear his own breath. He blew smoke out his nose. What he couldn't hear was the girl.

She had gone off behind a clump of bushes to pee, singing some half-remembered nursery rhyme to herself as she went. Once she disappeared around the bush the singing had stopped and he hadn't heard her since.

Of course, he would have to admit that for a few minutes he hadn't been paying much attention. He'd been thinking about the girl, right enough. Only he hadn't been thinking what he should have been thinking. Lots of thoughts had drifted across his mind, but the one that stayed the longest was the thought about the way her butt twitched in the moon-light. Earl had felt himself get hard then, but he was only thinking and it was dark, plus nobody was there to notice.

Now, however, it had been plenty long enough for Kathy to have done her business and he hadn't heard a peep. Damn, but that girl was one big lot of trouble. Probably a whole lot more trouble than she was worth.

Earl opened his eyes, took a final drag off his cigarette then ground it out against the trunk of the gum as he pushed off. "Kathy," he called. "Kathy, where are you?"

Only one of the owls answered back.

Damn it all anyway, Earl said to himself as he ambled toward the bushes she'd disappeared behind. Too damn bad if she was back there with her ass shining in the moonlight. Long enough was long enough.

The ground was uneven and he stumbled twice. Part of his clumsiness was due to the fact that he was still rather drunk. He could tell by the way trees and stars kept shifting in and out of focus. Why had he drunk so much? No doubt about it – he was a damn fool.

"Kathy, where are you? We need to be moving on. Come on out."

If she was behind the bushes, she didn't answer. Earl

parted branches and pushed through. All he could see was moonlight soaked ground, broken here and there by shifting shadows. He paused and listened, but even the owls had fallen silent.

He took another step, deeper into the shadows. Bugs whirled up from the tall grass and flung themselves against his face. The ground was uneven and he felt it give way under his left foot and then he was falling.

Earl flung his arms out, but all he grabbed were limber branches of bushes that gave way beneath his weight. The ground rose up and smacked him hard and he felt the air go whooshing out of his lungs. Then his head banged against something hard and he saw stars.

Everything went black and then it was all okay again, only he was lying on his back looking up at the stars. Something was wrong with them. They wouldn't quite hold still. They were wobbling on their points. A sour taste filled his mouth and his stomach churned. Earl wondered if he'd managed to give himself a concussion. Dumbass.

A giant pale moon swung slowly above his face. This moon smelled like crushed violets. Earl blinked and Kathy French swam into view. Her fingers drew a line across his forehead.

"Are you okay, Earl? That was a bad fall you took."

"Yeah, I'm fine. Only had the wind knocked out of me. And the only reason I fell was because I was trying to find you. If you'd come when I called none of this would have happened."

He could hear her laughing, only it sounded like she was far off. Then her hair was falling across his face and her arms slid around his neck.

"I was hoping you'd come find me, Earl. I wanted it to be you."

"Well, you got your wish. Now we've got to be rolling. Your aunt is waiting for you. She's bound to be getting worried."

"You know why I was hoping you'd find me, Earl? Huh? Do ya?"

Her breath was warm against his face. He could feel her body pressing against his. She was soft in all the right places for causing trouble.

"No," he said. "I don't know why and, furthermore, I don't want to know why. Now, ease back so I can get up."

The wind had come up again. He could hear it swooshing through the trees. Water ran over stones somewhere to his right. He could hear Kathy breathing. Her breath came in little gushes, like puffs of wind. Her hair ticked his cheeks. Her scent was strong, sweet and fresh, and it made Earl feel young again.

"I wanted it to be you so I could kiss you."

"Now, Kathy…"

"I've wanted to kiss you for a long time, Earl. I like to kiss big, strong men. You're sure a big, strong man."

"I'm also way too old for you and I'm supposed to be…"

Her lips pressed against his. He felt the tip of her tongue probing. For a moment Earl made his mouth hard. Then he felt it soften and he pulled the girl to him. It had been a damn long time since he'd kissed a woman. What could one kiss hurt?

Her fingers were busy with the buttons of his shirt and then she was pulling her dress over her head. Her breasts pressed out white and firm and perfect against the night. As though they had a will of their own, he felt his arms reaching for her. Her body molded into his arms. She smelled like violets.

Earl caught a glimpse of the stars. They were dancing

now. One drink too many, he thought. He could hear her breathing softly as he fumbled with his zipper. She moaned as he entered her, but it wasn't a sad sound. For a moment he could hear the murmuring of the water and the rising and falling of their breathing. It sounded like music. It sounded like the ocean at night.

Then her mouth was back against his and their bodies moved in rhythm. He could her quickening breathing and then he quit listening and started thrusting harder. Kathy's breath was soft and warm against his face as her scent mingled with the scent of honeysuckle in bloom. Her tongue was something wet and alive in his mouth and her hair swung before his face like a moving curtain. Once, through a gap, he saw stars. They were whirling like tiny silver dancers. A pot-bellied moon was watching.

Chapter 8

HIS FACE was cool and damp and he couldn't figure out why. To be honest, Earl wasn't positive where he was. For sure he was lying on something hard and lumpy. His eyes were closed, but light was seeping in. He blinked his eyes open.

He was outside, lying on the ground. It wasn't quite daylight, but morning was definitely a promise. Pale, pre-dawn light was filtering through the treetops and birds were chirping, only softly and irregularly as if they weren't quite awake themselves.

What the hell was he doing lying on the ground? And where in the hell had the night gone? Something was nibbling on his right ass check and Earl rolled over and scratched at whatever was chawing on him. Chiggers probably, or fleas. That was the way his luck had been running.

Nearby, somebody moaned and Earl felt his gut tighten. Who the hell was watching him? He rotated his head slowly. If it was some of the other police officers he was in for it.

For a minute he didn't see anything. Then he heard the

soft moaning again and his eyes followed the sound.

"Oh, shit," he said, not realizing he had spoken. There she was, Kathy French, naked as the day she was born, lying flat on her back, smiling in her sleep.

Memories began to filter to the surface. Jagged and incomplete as hell, but not incomplete enough. He knew better than to drink on an empty stomach, not that he ever held his liquor very well. What the hell had he done?

Had they done it? Earl strained to remember. Then wished he hadn't.

The mayor's daughter. The freaking mayor's daughter. The mayor's daughter who wasn't quite right. Now he was in so much trouble. Damn, damn, dirty damn.

Somewhere down the road toward town a pickup rumbled to life. Which is what the hell he'd better be doing, Earl figured. He'd screwed up before. Earl would be the first to admit that. But this time he had fudged up royally.

If he was real smart he'd just slip away before Sleeping Beauty woke up, then swear she'd run away from him and he'd never found her. Everybody in town knew Kathy French wasn't quite right.

Twenty years ago that might have worked. But today, with all the DNA tests, he knew old Earl would be on the wrong side of the bars inside a week. Dirty damn, what in the hell was he going to do?

Whatever it was he'd better do it fast. Daylight was coming hard now. He could see the tops of the trees clearly and make out the colors of the flowers blooming on the knoll to his right.

During the night they'd somehow wandered onto a ridge crest. The ground fell away on three sides into a deep swale that ran for maybe thirty yards below the crest of the ridge. The slope they'd come up wasn't as steep, but most of it was covered by brambles and sassafras saplings. Johnson grass and milkweed grew thick between the brambles. If there was a path, Earl couldn't see it. How the hell had they gotten through that mess? Not that it really mattered. What mattered was that they had to get out and then back to the truck. Not that getting to the truck would do much for Earl. He couldn't see a good way forward.

Off to the south a long moaning whistle blew, and Earl knew the early morning freight was starting up. Hauling dishwashers, stoves, and refrigerators from the Kenmore plant all the way to the coast. He wished like hell he was on that train.

The whistle blew again and Earl pushed himself off the ground and started walking toward the figure sprawled on the ground beside a blackberry bush. The bush was thick with purple-black berries and Earl's mouth watered. As he labored across the slope his stomach growled at him and he tried to remember when he'd eaten.

Halfway there, her blonde head rose from the earth like some new creature being born. Kathy French yawned, stretched, and smiled at him.

"Morning, Earl."

"Morning," he said, wondering what to say next.

"Did we make a baby last night?"

"Damn, Kathy, how the hell should I know? I sure hope not," he added.

A frown creased her face and her eyes bunched close together, making her appear slightly cross-eyed. Earl thought of one of his mother's favorite sayings, "What if your face freezes like that?" He wished it would happen to Kathy French. At least for a few days. Teach her a lesson.

"I thought you wanted us to make a baby, Earl."

"You sure got that wrong."

"But last night you said you did."

"I was liquored up last night. You can't put any stock in what I said then."

Kathy pushed out her fat lower lip. "I thought you liked me, Earl Turner."

"Ah, come on, Kathy, of course I like you. Only right now I've got to get you to your aunt's. She must be out of her mind with worry. Probably has called the cops by now. So get your clothes on. We've got to get rolling, and while we heading to your aunt's we've got to decide on a story."

"Not till you kiss me."

"Damn, Kathy, hurry up before somebody sees you naked."

She shrugged her freckled shoulders. "Nobody can see us. We're too far from the road. Besides, see if I care. Now, you had better kiss me, or else."

Earl most definitely didn't want to know what or else meant, so he bent and pecked at her cheek.

"No, sir. I want a kiss right on the lips. Just like we were married. Do you want to marry me, Earl?"

"All right, all right, I'll kiss you on the mouth. Only don't talk about marriage. No, no, not marriage," he mumbled as he bent and pressed his lips against hers. Earl had to admit Kathy French was a good kisser.

Earl licked his lips. They were still moist from her mouth. "Okay, Kathy, you've had your kiss. We really need to get the heck out of here. How much farther is it to your aunt's?"

Kathy giggled, a high-pitched, tinkling sound that grated on Earl's nerves. "About three hundred miles."

"What the hell are you talking about? Three hundred miles, my ass. Last night you said she lived just down the road a few miles."

"I was just kidding. She lives way over in Louisiana, clear

almost to Texas." She reached up and stroked one side of Earl's face with her fingertips. "She used to live out this road, though. But she moved about two years ago when Uncle Bert got transferred. He's in the oil business, you know."

"No I didn't know and what the hell were you thinking, Kathy? Damn it to hell, girl. Why did you lie to me? Do you know how damn deep in the shit we are? Or at least I am." He kicked at a patch of white daises and sent petals flying. "Shit, shit, shit. How stupid can you get?"

Kathy sobbed and turned her head, covering her face with her hands. "Don't yell at me, Earl. I was only kidding you."

Earl spun on his heel and looked off across the brambles and berry bushes. Between two sassafras bushes he could see a glimpse of pavement. Yelling at the girl wouldn't get him out of the hole he'd dug. Why in the hell had he started drinking anyway? Alcohol was nothing but trouble for him and he knew it. But still he drank. Why?

Thinking about his drinking reminded Earl of a story he'd heard one time. A man is walking down a street and there is a big hole in the road. The man falls in the hole. The next day the man is walking down the street and he knows the hole is there, but he falls in again. The third day the same man is walking down the street again and he knows the hole is there and he tells himself he is not going to fall in, but he does. The fourth day the man walks down a different street. But that was just a story and Earl knew he just kept falling in the same holes. It wasn't like he was totally stupid, so why did he do that?

Earl shook his head and blew out air he hadn't realized he'd been holding. "Okay, okay, I'm sorry I yelled at you. Now come on, Kathy, we really need to get you home. I'll think of something to tell your mom and dad. If they don't shoot me first."

Before he could turn, he felt a smooth, small hand slide against his right palm. Kathy's fingers squeezed his. That made him feel kind of funny. Like they were some old couple out for an early morning stroll.

"I know what we can do, Earl."

His head was hurting and he rubbed his left hand across his temples. Neck deep in all this shit and a hangover to boot. What had he done to deserve such a predicament? Talk about being behind the eight ball.

Oh, well, he'd just have to soldier through it, one step at a time. He'd done that before, during football practice, in the army, night shifts....

"And what can we do, Kathy?"

She smiled up at him, showing her teeth. They looked large to Earl, but what did he know about women's teeth. At least they looked clean.

"You take me home and I'll slip in the back door. I have a key." With her free hand she pulled a chain from beneath her dress. A brass key dangled at the end. "Then, if they're up early, I'll tell them I spent the night at Trudy Johnston's house. I've done that before, see? Anyway, they probably won't ask as long as I'm home and in bed before they get up. What do you think, Earl? Don't you think that's a good idea?"

"I don't know," Earl said. To tell the truth, he didn't think much of the idea. Surely Kathy's parents were more concerned about her than she let on. After all, she was their daughter. Plus, she wasn't quite right. Not bad enough for a home, but not fully loaded, either. Trouble was, he couldn't think of a better idea. Getting in the truck and driving to the Pacific Ocean wasn't exactly in the cards.

He looked down at Kathy. Then he took a long look toward the highway, toward town, toward what was surely going to be trouble, most likely the worst trouble of his troubled life.

"All right," he said, "let's try your idea. Only we've got to be going now." He turned and started off down the slope, tugging her along behind him.

Halfway down the slope, he noticed the quality of the light had changed. Daylight was upon them. Earl pushed on through the brambles and horseweeds. Behind him, he could hear Kathy fussing, jabbering away like some pissed off mynah bird. He could hear the sounds, but not the words. Tell the truth, he didn't much care what she was saying. All he could think of was getting to the truck, then getting her home.

If only no one saw them. He'd take the back streets and it was early, but still. With the way his luck had been running he hardly had a chance. Dear Lord, but he needed a break.

Earl could see the truck now and he plowed across the ditch and up onto the asphalt, jerking on the girl's arm, tugging her up the bank, taking no heed of her protests. Already the top of the cab was slashed with sunlight. Dear Lord, but he needed a break.

If he'd thought it'd have done one bit of good, he'd have prayed. But Earl Turner's prayers had never been answered and he didn't see any reason why they would be now. A cardinal flashed out of a cedar thicket on the far side of the road and streaked down the road, a red arrow winging west.

Chapter 9

SHADOWS STILL wreathed the corner of Sumpter and Mitchell. The truck idled along the curb beneath an oak that must have been alive when Sherman had taken Atlanta. Earl had the window down and he could hear birds chirping. He couldn't remember when he'd felt that cheerful.

"All right now, Kathy, you've got your key?"

"Right here." She pointed between her breasts. Earl tried not to think about how full and firm they were; he was already in enough trouble.

"And you're sure you can get in the back? I mean they don't have a deadbolt on the door, or anything like that?"

Kathy shook her head. "Nope, just a regular old lock. It kinda sticks sometimes, but I know how to unlock it."

Earl shook his head. This was going to go so wrong, he knew it, he just knew it.

Why in the name of all that was good and holy had he touched the first sip the night before? He could scream. In fact, if his head hadn't felt like it was made of cracking pond ice on the first warm day of spring he would have. Really, there ought to be a better way than this back door sneaking. But, if there was, he couldn't think of it.

Across the street a light flickered on in a small frame house. He was flat out of time. He turned to the girl. "Time to go, Kathy," he said, trying to keep his voice low and smooth and gentle. If there was one thing he didn't need it was for the goofy girl to go on a crying jag.

She didn't move. His stomach was growing queasier by the moment. Earl leaned across her and popped the door. A breeze swirled in and he could smell bacon frying. Every second was precious now.

"You've really got to go, Kathy."

She turned then, facing him at an angle, as though she couldn't get a true view straight on. "Earl?"

"What, Kathy?" Earl could hear the thread of irritation in his voice. He hoped the girl couldn't. Getting her upset wouldn't help a damn thing.

"Earl Turner, do you think we made a baby last night?"

Earl flung his head back against the cab wall and shut his eyes. "How the hell should I know?"

"You don't have to get mad, Earl. I just thought maybe we did. I mean you really got excited and all. You know you got really hard down there."

Earl groaned. Maybe his head would split open and spare him any more misery.

"What's the matter, Earl, don't you want to make a baby? If we're going to have a baby then we can get married. That's the way it works."

His stomach churned and his eyes popped open. "What do you mean that's the way it works?"

Kathy giggled again. Earl groaned again. That was one sound he truly was beginning to hate.

"That's how Margie Taylor and Beth Sullivan both got

married. They had sex with a boy and then they got big with a baby and the baby's daddy had to marry them. That's the way it works, Earl. Don't you know anything? Thought you would know about stuff like that. I mean, you being a grownup, and a policeman, and all."

Earl put his head in his hands. "No," he mumbled, "I don't know anything, not one damn thing." He could hear the birds chirping and he could smell bacon frying, but they didn't cheer him up one iota, and he was a big bacon man who had nothing against birds. No sir, if anybody ever found out about the night before it would be his ass frying.

Over on Bennett a car motor turned over. The morning was growing old and he'd aged ten years since he woke up. At this pace, he wouldn't last the week.

"Go on, Kathy, please. Before your mom and dad wake up."

"Not till you kiss me."

Earl gnawed on his tongue. What he felt like doing was screaming. He surely did not want to kiss Kathy French. Not here. Not in so much light. The lousy town was eaten up with busybodies, old men and women who had nothing better to do than poke their noses into other people's business. He didn't like anybody knowing his business.

"Kiss me, Earl Turner, or I won't go."

There was no use arguing. She would only cry, or worse, scream. He leaned over and pecked at her cheek.

"No, honey. On the lips. We're practically married. Kiss me like you should."

What I should do is kick her ass to the curb and start driving like my ass was on fire, he thought. But he didn't do it. What could he do? This time he'd got his ass in a real bind.

Short of murder, or suicide, he didn't see a way out. He'd have to get off somewhere to himself and do some long, hard thinking. Marriage was no picnic, period. Marriage to Kathy French would be a death sentence. He'd always wondered why some police officers put the business end of their service revolvers in their mouth. Now he knew.

Earl leaned over and kissed the girl on the mouth. That part wasn't unpleasant. He couldn't pretend it was. He didn't like doing it in broad daylight, though. But what choice did he have?

To his surprise, the girl smiled, slid out of the car, and started sashaying toward her house. Women, he'd never understand them. Not if lived to be as old as Methuselah. He bet Methuselah had never been married. Not and lived almost a thousand years.

Earl watched the girl walk down the sidewalk, swinging her arms like some schoolgirl. Already he felt a hundred years old. Just before she turned the corner, she looked back and waved. Earl saluted, then shifted into reverse. Visions of disaster buzzed in his head like angry hornets.

Chapter 10

DAYLIGHT WAS breaking full bore by the time he cut off the main highway and rolled down Turner's Branch for the final two mile run to the house. The possibility that both his folks had slept in was somewhere between slim and none and he dreaded the conversation.

His mother was bad to ask twenty questions when one would suffice and as for his dad, well it was safe to say the old man's mouth got a little smarter each day. As he sped around the corner where the school bus had rolled and crashed Earl's junior year, he thought about Amy Wilson. She'd only been fifteen. He gunned the motor up the slope, eased off the gas, and swung wide into the driveway.

Tall grass along the drive slow-danced in the rising morning breeze and glittering dewdrops looked like tears. Well, tears were about right. If he hadn't been a grown man, he'd have shed a few.

Earl glanced up the drive and, just like he'd figured, there was his old man, sitting in a pool of sunlight on the back porch steps, a coffee cup in one hand and a cigarette in the other. Last year, after he developed a cough that didn't want to leave, the old man had tried to quit smoking. That effort had lasted less than a week and made him grouchy as hell. Earl goosed the gas and sent gravel flying. Might as well make an entrance.

As he drove over the cattle guard, Earl eased off the accelerator and tapped the brake. The truck rolled to a stop in front of what his old man called the tool shed. The name must have been a holdover from when his dad was a kid. For as long as Earl could remember the building had stood empty, except for wasps and spiders, peeling paint and leaning south on its foundation another degree or two each year. Ninety percent of the paint had peeled off years ago and rotten wood glared like cancer sores. Two summers before, Earl had tried to get his dad to let him tear the shed down, but the old man had flat refused, starting a two-day argument. Earl shook his head, cut the engine, and popped the door.

A clutch of his mother's Rhode Island Reds were pecking the ground. Earl kicked at the dust around their feet and they scattered in all directions, clucking loudly. If only all his troubles would scatter so quickly.

Sweat worms crawled across his scalp, but his insides felt like ice. His stomach churned slowly and he wondered if he was going to be sick. Earl dug his handkerchief out of his back pocket and wiped the sweat off his forehead.

"Boy, you look like something the cat drug in. Rough night?"

Earl glanced at his father, then looked off across the fields. In the early morning light the corn tassels were golden. "Not really."

Okay, that was a lie, but what business was it of his old man, or anybody else, what he did. He was a grown man and the rest of the world just needed to let him be.

"Well, hate to say this, son, but you look like forty miles of bad road."

The old man took a drag on his cigarette and let the smoke slide out the corner of his mouth. "Not to mention you smell like a distillery."

"I had a beer or two."

"And then drove? And you a police officer?"

Earl didn't say anything. What was there to say? Even if there had been a good response he knew he'd be wasting his breath. The old man flat out liked to argue, and the subject didn't matter. Only he'd call it discussing.

As long as Earl could remember his dad had been argumentative. Only the last few years he'd gotten worse. Retirement hadn't suited Oscar Turner. Time seemed to hang heavily and awkwardly on him, like a too large wool coat that had been soaked in salt water. His dad often seemed to be shifting under its weight.

The old man should have stayed on at the mill, instead of taking the buyout. Earl wasn't figuring on hanging up his badge anytime soon. Distorted lyrics from an old country song meandered through his mind – killing time is killing me.

Off to the north a calf called for its mother, and Earl turned and let his eyes drift across the corn tassels waving in the early morning breeze and the line of black locust that marked a fence row. Beyond the trees was a field of soybeans and then the land rose slowly, like bread rising, to an upland meadow of wildflowers and tall grasses shifting in the wind. One day he'd start walking and see what was on the other side of that field, and then what was beyond that.

"You not speaking to your father this morning?"

Earl jerked at the sound of his father's voice. Drifting again, he thought, daydreaming. That was going to get him in big trouble. Earl almost laughed. He was in so much trouble already that a little more couldn't make much difference.

Earl coughed and spat out some of the crud lining his lungs. This was one hell of a morning. His pulse throbbed in his temples. "What do you want me to say?"

He could see the old man giving him the eye. That's what he called it when his dad looked at him out of the corners of his eyes. Looked at him like he was the afterbirth of a Mongolian Bang-Bang. Yeah, he'd disappointed the old fart. But what the hell, the old man had disappointed him plenty of times.

"Nothing in particular, was just wondering what was on your mind?"

"Nothing's on my mind, nothing."

Inside the house the telephone rang, once, twice, then fell silent. Earl could hear the clucking of hens and the faint hum of a mowing machine moving across some field off to the south, probably the McBride place. An early morning slant of sun warmed one side of his face and he could smell bacon frying in the kitchen. The rose of Sharon bush was in bloom by the door and the scattered clouds were outlined in gold. All Earl was trying to do was keep from vomiting.

The voice of his father brought him back. "Just thought you looked like you had something on your mind."

Earl wiped his mouth with the back of his hand and tried to focus on the grape arbor that ran between the side of the house and the storm cellar. Norton grapes grew there; his father had ordered them from one of his seed catalogs twenty years before. The vines never produced much, but they grew thick and green and it was cool in their shade.

Earl could feel his brain spinning like one of those centrifuge devices he'd seen on the news. He closed his eyes tightly, but then he could see pinpricks of yellow shooting off in all directions. "Guess, I'm just thinking about going to bed. It was a night."

Earl waited a moment, but his father didn't say any more. He turned then and started walking slowly toward the kitchen door. The hum of the mowing machine reverberated inside his brain. At least it wasn't a vision of Kathy French. The sooner he forgot about that girl the better. Thank God, she wasn't quite right. If she'd been a normal girl he'd have already been in it up to his neck. On second thought – he probably already was.

Chapter 11

EARL TURNED left on yellow and wheeled into the parking lot. Leaves scurried across the asphalt, pushed by a northwest wind. Earl maneuvered between the white lines, cut the motor, popped the door, and slid out of his truck. The air that greeted him was cool enough to make him wish for a jacket.

An early fall seemed in the offing. Earl liked fall: the cooler temperatures, the changing color of the leaves, the return of football. It was what followed fall that he hated.

A guy named Steinbeck had written a novel called *The Winter of our Discontent*. Earl couldn't remember why now, but years ago he'd read at it. The storyline he'd forgotten, but the title had stuck in his brain and returned each year with the first blast of cool air after the sauna of summer. Earl trudged across the parking lot and pushed the station house door open.

"Chief wants to see ya, Earl."

Earl nodded and kept walking. He didn't want to talk to Joe Barr. The man was a real loser. One of those wanna-be cops who don't have the balls to take it to the street. For as long as Earl had worked for the department, Joe Barr had been a combination desk man, receptionist, and dispatcher. Earl had to admit the man worked a lot of hours, but he couldn't see where Barr's work amounted to much.

Oh, being a dispatcher was all right, and every police department had to have one, but the rest of what the man did was merely paperwork and answering the phone. Earl shook his head. Working a job like that would drive him crazy, although some days he wondered if he wasn't already halfway there.

The break room was empty, which suited Earl fine. He didn't care much for his fellow officers; he certainly wasn't fishing buddies with any of them. Tell the truth, he wasn't sure where most of them lived. Dave Baker's house he knew, but only because they'd been in the same class all the way through school.

Before he could see the coffee, he could smell it. Only a puddle at the bottom of the glass pot and starting to scorch. He poked the OFF button and poured what coffee there was into a cup that might have been clean. The coffee would be nasty as hell, but he needed the kick. Especially since he had to see the chief. What the hell had he done now?

Earl blew on his coffee. The last night he'd worked he hadn't even pulled anybody over and then he'd been off three straight shifts. Probably somebody complaining about a ticket he'd given them. People in Denton were always trying to get out of something: paying a speeding ticket, paying their taxes, their kid out of a possession charge, their marriage. Earl took a cautious sip. Damn, the stuff was nasty. He sipped again then headed for the chief's office.

The sign on the desk was the kind employees buy for their boss after he'd been on the job twenty years, carved out of walnut, with swirls, curlicues, and designs of leaves and flowers etched on the front, with the nameplate done in brass and screwed to the sign: *Chief Evans*.

The chief was sitting at his desk, scribbling on a watch report. He was bent over and his bald spot was visible. Seeing the top of his chief's head like that embarrassed Earl.

Baldness wasn't something most men cared for, unless they were like that actor, Yul Brenner, or those skinheads you saw in prisons. Earl shivered. Those guys were dangerous as hell. He'd talked to enough prison guards to know skinheads were worse than wild animals. A wild animal, a bear or a cougar, would kill for food or to protect its territory. Skinheads, however, killed because they liked killing. Killing and maiming and raping and torturing.

Why last year, two of them out on parole had gouged a preacher's eyes clear out of his head with a Phillips screwdriver. When the cops interrogated them, the bastards told the officers they did it to show the preacher what a pussy his God was. Earl shivered again and rapped his knuckles on the chief's door.

"Come in."

Earl studied the chief's face as he lifted his head. The chief was a hard man to read. Usually the chief had a smile for his men, but that didn't always mean much. The chief nodded at the wooden chair in front of his desk and Earl sat down.

The chief leaned back in his chair and showed Earl a few dingy teeth. One in the front was chipped. "You just getting back?"

"Got back last evening."

"Heard you went fishing."

Earl nodded. He couldn't see where this was going. Maybe there wasn't a problem. Maybe the chief only wanted to talk about fishing. Yeah, maybe.

"Where'd you go, Carnico?"

"Nope, went down to Buena Vista. Heard the bass were biting."

The chief leaned forward. "Catch many?"

Earl eased back in his chair. He felt like putting his feet up on the chief's desk. "A few. Did get one really nice large-mouth. Went just over fourteen."

"That is a nice one. I'm a catfish man, myself."

"They're good eating."

"Yep, they are. Wish I had me a mess of them now." The chief grinned. "With hush puppies."

The chief leaned forward and rubbed one hand along the back of his neck. For the first time, Earl thought his boss looked like an old man. Earl felt sorry for him. Then it occurred to him he wasn't getting any younger either.

The chief closed his eyes, as if he was going to sleep. Earl really felt uncomfortable, so he looked out the small window to the right of the desk. A woman was walking a dog on the sidewalk.

The woman was tall and wore a blue sweater. Something in the set of her shoulders put Earl in mind of Evelyn Gilchrest, a girl he'd gone to school with. They'd had a pair of dates back in high school, the movies once and then a church picnic one summer. He could still remember the taste of the homemade banana ice cream. Earl felt himself smiling. Traffic hummed on the street and sunlight poured through the window and splattered on the stained carpet.

The chief coughed softly and Earl wiped the smile off his face with the back of one hand.

"Earl, I had a call yesterday."

All right, Earl thought, here it comes. Somebody bitching about something I've done. Why the hell didn't people just pay their tickets?

"And…"

The chief rearranged his face. "And it was the mayor."

"Mayor French?"

The chief shook his head like Earl was a schoolboy who had just missed an easy question on a pop quiz.

"Like how many mayors do we have in this town, Earl?"

Earl shrugged. He didn't say anything. He had a real bad feeling where this conversation was going. So bad he half expected the chief to read him his Miranda rights.

"All right then, I'll tell you. We've got one. A certain Mr. William Emerson French. And he's the mayor, Earl, which makes him your boss, and mine."

"Okay, I know who the mayor is, Chief."

"Well, good, we're making progress here. Now do you know why he called me?"

"Because his wife got a ticket?" Earl grinned to show the chief he was kidding. But he knew he was only kidding himself.

"No, damn it, the mayor didn't call because his wife got a ticket." The chief rubbed at the anger lines in his face. He rubbed with a certain vigor, but the effort didn't change much. "He called because his daughter is pregnant."

The chief turned and stared out the window. Earl glanced out the window, too, but he didn't see much worth looking at. However, he had to admit, he wasn't concentrating at the moment, except on the twisting in his gut.

The chief swiveled in his chair. "Now, you may be wondering why the mayor felt obliged to call the chief of police to let him know that his daughter was pregnant."

"None of my business," Earl said.

"Oh, really? Well, Mr. Earl Turner, it may interest you

greatly to know that the mayor says the man who got his un-married, slightly special daughter pregnant is an officer on this very force."

Earl killed the rest of his coffee. It was going cold and was bitter as poison. His guts were churning like the Gulf with a hurricane blowing in. "Who's he claiming is the daddy?"

"Well now, Earl, it's real funny you should ask that question, because the mayor said his daughter was crystal clear on the officer's name. Said she didn't even stutter one time. You wanna guess who that outstanding protector of the public might be?"

Earl was tempted to say Gary Woodson or Tom Underwood, but he knew the shit had hit the fan and being a smart ass was only going to make everything worse. He could sense his mind racing trying to figure a way out.

"Now, Chief, how would I know?"

Earl couldn't look the chief in the eye. He knew that wasn't good, but he also knew if he did the chief would read him like the Atlanta phone book. So he kept his eyes averted, looking first at the floor, then out the window. After a bit, he risked a quick glance at the chief out of the corner of one eye – just in time to see the chief shaking his head.

"Don't give me any bullshit, Earl."

"What do you mean?"

"I mean Kathy French says you're the man who did the dirty deed. Now what do you say to that?"

"Now, Chief, you know that girl isn't quite right."

"She may not be the brightest bulb in the box, but she's sure got her daddy and mother convinced that you are the man. And we both know who for sure who her daddy is."

"Okay, so he's the mayor. What the hell does that have to do with me?"

"What it means is that he's got the clout to make things very hot for you, and me. Whole damn department as a matter of fact."

The chief banged the palms of his hands on the top of his desk. Earl twitched like he'd been tased.

"Now, Officer Turner, you know what the real kicker is?"

Earl shook his head. He didn't have a clue. From the tone of the chief's voice, he didn't want to have a clue.

"You know, I don't believe you do. And you know why? Because if you did you'd be sweating mortar and shitting bricks."

The chief made a funny noise in the back of his throat, then pushed up out of his chair. To Earl the noise sounded like a cross between a choked-off laugh and a sob. The chief walked over to the window and stared out at the street. At least Earl figured he was staring out at the street. Since the chief had his back to him, he could have had his eyes closed for all Earl knew.

The chief simply stood there with his back to Earl. He didn't say a word, not a single, lousy word. The silence seemed to come alive, like a ghost or a zombie. Certain old timers still believed in spirts and hoodoo. Earl didn't really believe in such, but he had seen a few things on the graveyard shift he couldn't explain.

The office had grown quiet. Earl could hear Compton's delivery truck roll by and the cardinal in the cedar outside the office. He could hear the telephone ringing down the hall and a murmur of voices from the two old ladies strolling down the sidewalk. He could even hear the faint hum of the fluorescent lights and the fainter wheeze of his own breathing. It sounded like something out a movie. Earl wished today was a movie.

"Earl, I've always sorta liked you. Not sure why exactly,

but I've always had a soft spot for you. Maybe it's because you remind me of my nephew, Jaspar. You might have heard of him. Good kid, just kept stepping in it. Doing eighteen months at Colby at the moment." The chief shook his head. "Receiving stolen property, the big dummy."

He whirled on his toes then, spinning around like a younger man. Earl remembered the chief had been an all-conference guard in high school. The chief leaned back against the glass, crossed his arms and stared straight at Earl's face. Earl felt the sweat starting up along the back of his neck. He wished he'd never come back from the lake.

"Kathy French is pregnant, Earl." The chief showed Earl some of his teeth in what might have passed for a grin if a man was truly open-minded. "And she's telling the whole wide world you're the daddy."

Chapter 12

EARL BLINKED and felt his mind swirl back inside his skull. He'd been drifting across deep space. For a heartbeat, maybe two, he wasn't sure where he was, or even who he was. Then something clicked in his brain and he knew. What the hell was he going to do now? Why had he ever gone to the stupid party?

"What's the matter, Earl, you speechless?"

Earl rubbed his face with the palm of his left hand – he didn't want the chief reading anything from his expressions. At the moment, he simply didn't trust himself. It was hard to put on a poker face when you'd just been gut punched.

"Now, Chief, you know me…"

"I thought I did, but this sure throws all that out the window. Hellfire, Earl, I knew you weren't Prince Charming, but I never figured you for this. Sure, you might be a little rough with a drunk or cuss out a preacher. But raping the mayor's daughter?"

Earl felt his bones slamming together. He half rose out of his chair. "Now hold it right there. I've never raped anybody in my life and I sure as hell don't intend to start now."

"But you did do the dirty deed with Kathy French?"

Earl eased back down in his chair. He was starting to sweat, but still he felt chilled clear to his bones. Maybe he was coming down with some dreadful fever and would die before morning. At least all his troubles would be over then.

"We might have kissed some, maybe fooled around a little." Earl shrugged. He put his best good-old-boy smile on his face and looked the chief dead in the eye. Maybe he could still pull his nuts out of the fire. "Might have had a drink or two. Can't claim I'm crystal on all the details."

The chief didn't smile and Earl felt his guts start to curdle.

Chief Evans shook his head sadly. Earl could tell the old boy was disappointed in him. "So what you're saying, Officer Turner, is that you got drunk at a party, then proceeded to get behind the wheel and drove drunk, endangering not only yourself, but your passenger, who just happened to be the mayor's special needs daughter, not to mention any other poor unsuspecting soul who just happened to be out on the highway that night. Then…"

"Now, Chief, I…"

Evans held one hand up. "Let me finish, Officer Turner."

Earl sighed and settled back in his chair. He didn't care for that Officer Turner shit. Going formal was a damn bad sign.

"As I was saying, then you proceed to take this innocent young girl…"

"She's not that young. I know for a fact…"

"Officer Turner, I said let me finish."

"Yes, sir." Earl sat up straight and assumed his best Academy classroom face.

"All right now, let's try this again." Chief Evans leaned forward and pointed his beak straight at Earl. "Now as I was saying, you drive this innocent young girl to a remote location in the middle of the night where you proceed to rape her."

"Now, damn it to hell…"

"Shut the fuck up, Earl, and let me finish. One more interruption out of you and your ass is suspended for two weeks, without pay. We clear on that point?"

Earl nodded. If it meant keeping his job he'd never even whisper in front of the chief again. Besides, he'd caught that comment about a two-week suspension. If the chief had been going to can his ass he wouldn't have mentioned a suspension.

"Good. Now you proceed to rape the girl, ask her to lie about it, then basically abandoned her by the side of the road."

Earl bit his lip. Dropping a girl off two blocks from her home was hardly abandoning her by the side of the road. But he needed the job, so he bit his lip and tried to look like an officer on the cover of *Police Gazette*.

The chief leaned back in his chair and let air seep out between his thin lips like they were halves of a tire sidewall that had just been punctured. He rubbed at his forehead as if he were trying to massage some semblance of feeling back into it. Finally, he lifted his head and peered at Earl. Earl wondered why the old man was looking at him. He'd seen Earl a thousand times and Earl knew he wasn't anything special to look at. He didn't even like to look at himself in the mirror.

"Guess by now you're asking yourself what the hell we're going to do about this mess you've created."

Earl nodded. He liked the sound of we. Maybe the chief had a plan. He sure as shit could use one right now.

"Good. I'm glad you're beginning to appreciate the hole

you've dug for yourself." The chief twisted his head on his neck until he was looking at Earl only out of the sides of his eyes. He looked vaguely like the picture of a pigeon Earl had seen once in a *National Geographic*. The pigeon had been garroted.

"Now, I've been laying the bad news on you pretty hard, but there is some good news."

Well, let's hear it, Earl thought. He kept his mouth shut, though. Today was not his time to talk.

"About the only break we've caught so far is that Mayor French hasn't been inclined to go around town blabbing everything he knows about this situation. Reckon he isn't thrilled with the idea of the whole town knowing his daughter is knocked up."

"Well, that sounds better. Maybe he'll just send her away for a little while…"

"Send her away?"

"Yeah," Earl said, "you know sometimes when a girl gets in the family way, well the family doesn't make a big deal out of the situation. Instead, they simply have the girl go away for a few months and when she comes back everything is all right."

"You mean there is no baby?"

Earl nodded. He was glad the chief was figuring it out. He hated having to explain things to people, especially the chief. The boss could be real thick at times.

"Let me see if I understand you, Earl. So a girl gets pregnant, then goes away and has an abortion and comes back home and everything is just fine?"

"Well, sometimes they give the baby away. You know, to somebody that wants a child. Like a couple who can't get, you know…" Earl could hear the words trailing off, dying in his throat. He didn't like to talk all that much, period. Let alone try and make somebody understand something. Most especially he didn't like talking about anything to do with sex, and babies were surely tied up with the sex thing. Both sides of his neck were warming up and he figured he was blushing. He tried again.

"Like the couple wants a baby but can't have one for some reason, so they adopt. So like it works out great for everybody."

"Always got the answer, don't you Turner?"

"No, not always." What in the world was ragging the chief now?

The chief slapped his desk with one hand. Earl twitched. He'd bet twenty bucks the chief would rather have slapped him than the desk.

"Well, that's real good, cause this is one of those times when it ain't going to work that way. I've got that straight from the source and you can take it to the bank and stuff it in your lockbox." The chief leaned closer. "Want to know how it's going to work, Officer Turner?"

Earl didn't think he wanted to know anything more, but he also didn't see where he had a choice. Sure, he would have liked to have told the chief where to get off, but he valued his job. So he nodded. He didn't like it, but he nodded.

"That's the right answer. Now listen good, Earl. I mean listen real good. There's only one way out of this maze and I'm only going to tell you once."

Chief Evans paused and ran the back of one hand across his mouth. His face looked like he'd just bitten down on a rotten apple.

"Ready?"

Earl nodded. His body was oozing sweat and his right knee jerked up and down like a pneumatic hammer. He wasn't sure if he could speak. So he looked out the window.

It felt like he was in prison.

"Good. Here it is. The mayor is crazy about his daughter and wants to do anything he can to make her happy, especially in her condition. Care to guess what Kathy French says is the only thing in the world that would make her happy? The only thing. Well?"

"No clue."

Earl watched the chief's lips curl into a grin. The old varmint looked worse than ever. How could any one man get so nasty looking in one life?

"Now, Earl, I'm right proud of you at this particular moment in time. You know why? No? Well, it's because for once in your sorry existence you are telling the truth, the whole truth, and nothing but the truth, so help you God. You really don't have a clue. Not one clue about the eighteen wheeler that is fixing to smash into you and grind you into the ground. No sir, you don't have a clue."

Chief Evans snorted. Maybe the sound was supposed to be a laugh, Earl thought. Whatever it was supposed to be, it made him sick at his stomach. It was the sound an animal might make. Earl tried to keep his face from showing anything. No use pouring kerosene on that fire.

"Well, Mister Love-em and Leave-em, here is your sentence. And yes, I have appointed myself judge, and the jury, a.k.a. Kathy French, says she wants nothing more in life than to marry the father of her child, who is you."

The chief roused himself then and stood behind his desk. He leaned forward and put the palms of his hands flat on smooth dark wood. His face was set in hard lines.

"Officer Earl Clark Turner, I hereby sentence you to a lifetime of wedded hell to Kathy Gail French, a nice enough girl, but dumber than dirt. May the Lord look over you two, cause you folks most assuredly are going to need all the help you can lay your hands on."

The chief paused, gnawed on his lower lip, then shook his head. "Now get out of my office before I fire your ass."

A flash of heat shot through his brain, but his bones felt cold and brittle, like March ice. Somehow Earl found himself on his feet. He wanted to say something, anything to protest the injustice that was being inflicted on him. He even opened his mouth. But no words came.

A moment later he turned and started for the door. The room looked a hundred yards long. His legs were wobbly and felt far away. The walls seemed to have tilted, as though sometime during the session the earth had shifted on its axis. Earl's head was spinning and for a moment he thought he was going to pass out.

Chapter 13

EARL WHEELED his truck into the driveway and cut the engine. The ping of the engine was harsh in the soft quiet of late Sunday afternoon. Early fall sunlight lay thick and heavy across still green lawns. Nothing moved: no dog, no cat, even the birds weren't flying.

Earl glanced at the sky. If there were any clouds he couldn't see them. With the smooth green lawns and old white homes fronted by oak and maple trees, the landscape looked like an Edward Hopper painting. Hopper was about the only painter he liked. Well there was Remington, but that was the old west and Earl was in the new south.

Damn, it was hot. He was flat out burning up. Wearing his suit had been a damn stupid idea. Who the hell was he trying to impress, anyway? The cards had been dealt and his flush had been busted clear to Vicksburg.

Plus, he'd had to lie to his mother about where he was going and why. Earl had never been one to wear suits except to funerals and church on Easter Sunday and Christmas Eve. Well, he hadn't told her a complete lie. He'd only left out chunks of truth.

He could feel the sweat coating his chest, dampening his hairline, and pooling in the small of his back. He felt like he'd wandered into a car wash by mistake. Sweat started sliding down his face and he tugged a handkerchief out of a hip pocket and mopped it up.

It was past time to be going in, but he simply couldn't make himself move. He'd have to, but he couldn't. For sure, he was in a monster of a mess. Worst he'd ever been in, and that was saying something.

The engine had quit pinging and it was like the day had died, or the earth had paused in the middle of its rotation. Earl could hear his own breathing and smell his sweat over the scent of the Old Spice he'd splashed on earlier.

Along with his sweat, he could smell something else. The other thing smelled like fear. Which didn't surprise Earl. The metallic taste of it was on his tongue. Sweat ran down the crack of his ass and he said seven of the worst words he knew and popped the door. The drive looked a mile long and his legs felt like concrete. He turned his head and spat some of the cotton out of his mouth and started putting one foot in front of the other.

It seemed a long walk up the driveway and, in a strange way, it reminded him of other walks. Not just any walk, but certain walks. He could almost name one, but the time and place were shrouded in smoke and mist. He was within ten feet of the front door when the memory clicked into place.

The memory walk was the one he'd taken after the loss in the regional his senior year. They'd been so close and he'd given everything he had. His entire body had ached liked he'd gone five rounds with a cement mixer and blood had still been seeping from the cut on the inside of his lip. One more play – all they had needed was one more play and they would have gone to the state quarterfinals. Making that walk back to the locker room liked to have killed him. Knowing the disappointment he would face there was almost more than he'd been able to stand. No one person ever won or lost a game alone, but he was the only one who'd fumbled inside the Montclair County three yard line with just under two minutes on the clock.

There were nights Earl wondered if his whole life would have been different if he'd cut back and dove for the end zone instead of trying to bull his way in.

Well, that had been one damn bad walk and this was another. He rang the doorbell.

Right away, Earl could hear a squeal of voices followed by footsteps echoing down the hall. The voices came closer. He could hear words now, muffled by the thick door. It was a door that would put up a fight. Earl had seen Tom Underwood break his wrist trying to smash in a door one night on a raid. He wiped a line of sweat off his forehead. His stomach was knotting up, hurting like he'd swallowed barbed wire.

Earl turned and looked down the driveway. Part of him wanted to start running and never look back. He took a deep breath and tried to clear his mind.

Before he could decide anything, he heard more voices and then the creak of the heavy door as it swung open. As he turned, Earl tried to fix some sort of a smile on his face.

Faces swam up to the light from the darkness of the vestibule. There was a smiling face, a stern face, and an uncertain face. Earl wondered what his face looked like.

For sure his face felt hot, flushed like he was running a fever, and there was a roaring in his ears. The faces inside the house were talking. He could see their lips moving, but all he could hear was a babbling of voices.

There was a passage in the Bible about a tower of Babel.

Earl remembered that much from his Sunday school days. He wished he could remember a really good prayer.

Earl knew the people were talking to him and that he needed to say something. He tried to mumble some sort of greeting, only his voice wasn't working quite right, so he just smiled bigger and started nodding.

"Oh, Earl, I'm so glad you came. It was getting kinda late and Daddy said you weren't coming and Mommy said dinner was getting cold and I was worried that something had happened to you, something bad."

Earl swallowed and felt his mind clear considerable. "Hi, Kathy," he said as he stuck out a hand toward the mayor. Earl still thought of the man as the mayor, not as his future father-in-law. He just couldn't. Even whispering father-in-law to himself in the dark made his stomach hurt worse.

Mayor French took his hand. Earl saw distaste flicker across the man's face. So his palm was sweaty. If the situations were reversed, Bill French's hand would be sweaty, too. Anybody's would. The mayor gave Earl a tight grip and shook his hand hard, once.

"You might as well come in."

Earl nodded and let go of the mayor's hand. Somehow, Kathy had got her arms all twisted up with his and they stumbled through the door sideways. This was going to be one helluva afternoon. Earl could see that, clear enough.

Out of the sunlight it was cooler and Earl was glad to stand in the dimly lit vestibule, letting his eyes adjust, trying to get his heart to quit pounding so hard. He dabbed at his damp forehead with a handkerchief that had been clean when he'd left his house.

After a moment, he looked around. The other three faces were staring at him. Only faint light from the dining room window penetrated the vestibule, so that the faces were half in shadow. Because he couldn't see them clearly, he couldn't read them, and that made Earl nervous. Nervous the same way stopping a car with tinted windows did. There just wasn't any way of knowing who was in the car. Shit could always happen.

Mrs. French tittered, sounding like a bird with a seed stuck in its throat. "So nice of you to come, Mr. Turner."

"Just call me Earl."

"All right, Earl. We're glad you could make it. Dinner is on the table. Shall we?"

Kathy made a squealing sound and her father mumbled something that Earl couldn't quite catch. He didn't say anything. Just allowed himself to be gently steered into the dining room.

The table was set with what looked like good china and the rims of the water goblets looked like gold, although Earl figured it was just some fancy paint. There were three forks and two spoons beside every plate and Earl wondered which one he was supposed to use when. He'd have to watch Kathy's mother and follow her lead.

"Now, I'll sit here, Earl and Kathy can sit here and, dear, you can…"

"I know where to sit, Sue." Mr. French ran his fingers through his silver hair. He surely looked like a politician, Earl thought.

Mayor French gave Earl a hard look, and then shifted the same look to his wife. "Okay, already, let's sit down. Damn roast is half-cold now. No use letting it get any colder."

Earl thought about holding the chair for Kathy. He'd seen men do that in movies. But then he wondered if shouldn't hold the chair for her mother. Before he could make up his mind the rest of them were already seated.

"For God's sake, Earl, sit down. You act like you've got

sunstroke."

Earl fumbled for the back of the chair. How had he gotten himself into such a mess? Never mind, Earl thought, that was one question he could answer. "Sorry."

"Well, you got that right."

"Bill."

"Now, Sue."

"Please, Bill, let's not fuss at the table." Mrs. French squinched her face up so that her eyes almost disappeared and smiled. "Will you say the blessing, honey?"

Mr. French grunted, but bowed his head. Earl closed his eyes. Without warning his stomach grumbled. In the sudden silence the noise sounded vaguely obscene. He heard Ms. French sigh. Kathy giggled. Earl figured, without question, this had to be just about the worst day of his life. For once he was glad to hear a prayer.

Chapter 14

EARL PUT down his fork and wiped his mouth. "That sure was good, Mrs. French."

"Yeah, Mom, it was really tasty."

"I hope you saved room for dessert. I've baked a sweet potato pie. Used my mother's recipe."

"Well…"

"Sue, we'll get to your pie later. Right now though we need to have a discussion." Mr. French thrust his head as far across the table as his neck would stretch. Earl thought the man looked like a snapping turtle.

"You ready for a little discussion, Earl?"

Earl nodded. He would rather eat a piece of pie and go home, but he'd known all along that wasn't in the cards. "Sure, let's talk."

"Wanna talk here, or the den?"

What difference did it make, Earl wondered. "The den," he said, just to exercise a little bit of control, even though he knew he had about as much control of the situation as a Dominicker hen in a tornado.

"All right, let's go." Mr. French pushed his chair back,

"I'm coming, too," Mrs. French said.

"And me," Kathy squealed.

Earl winced at the shrillness. Almost every time the girl spoke her voice grated on his nerves. How in the world was he going to survive? Marriage to her was a Chinese torture death sentence. Surely he could find a way out. Always before he'd found some way to escape bad trouble.

"No, this is between Earl and me."

"She's my daughter, too, Bill."

"Hard words may have to be said, Sue."

"So, I can take hard words. Haven't I heard them often enough? Besides, who went through all the pain of giving birth? It wasn't you, I promise you that."

Mr. French rolled his eyes at the ceiling. "Sue, you're missing the point."

"No, Bill, you are. Kathy is not just your daughter. She's our daughter and I'm going to be in on any conversation regarding her."

Bill French let out a big sigh. "All right, Sue, all right, you can sit in, but don't say I didn't warn you."

"Me, too. I'm coming, too."

"No, Kathy, absolutely not. I forbid it."

"Why not let her be part of all this, Bill?"

"She's too, er, well, too innocent. That's it, too innocent."

"Bill, think of what you're saying. Too innocent? Why she's already in the family way."

"But, Sue..."

"But nothing, Bill. This is about her, about her life. Of all the people in the world, she should be there. Don't you agree, Earl?"

Earl looked at Mr. French. Then he glanced at Mrs. French. He didn't look at Kathy. Earl didn't know what to say. If he answered one way he'd make Kathy's mother mad. Answer the other way and he'd hack off Kathy's dad. Anyway, what was there to say? Earl shrugged.

"You all can't talk about me if I'm not there. That's not right."

"Now, Kathy…"

"Daddy, if you don't let me come I'm going to cry and cry and cry."

Earl closed his eyes. Kathy's voice was so shrill it was like someone had started a drill inside his head. Without a shadow of a doubt, this had to be the worst mess of his life. If he'd thought prayer worked at all, he'd have said a big, long one. Damn, if the woman didn't stop carrying on his skull was going to crack.

"Now, Kathy…"

"Oh, come on, Bill, let's all go to your den. I'll fix us drinks."

Earl opened his eyes and swung his legs out from under the table. A drink sounded like one hell of a fine idea. A double would be twice as good. He felt Kathy's hand slip inside his and, just for the hell of it, he gave it a squeeze.

They trooped out of the dining room and marched down a short hallway. Photographs of what Earl figured were family members lined the walls. Most of the women had long, dark hair and pointed chins, while most of the men wore heavy, dark beards. They all looked rather ferocious.

One photo in particular caught Earl's attention. The man's hair and beard were black and wild, but it was his eyes that made the skin on the back of Earl's neck pucker. They were high and deep set, so light they looked hollow. It was like looking into the eyes of a ghost, a haunted ghost, Earl thought. He sure as hell wouldn't want to have pulled that man over for reckless driving.

There were two high-backed easy chairs and a settee in the den. Mr. French took one chair and Mrs. French took the other. That left the settee for him and Kathy, although for a minute Earl toyed with the idea of just leaning against the big Sony TV that lounged in a corner. Standing would give him a better sense of control of the situation, but Kathy patted the settee and her dad gave him a long hard look, so Earl sat down. Control wasn't in the cards on this one.

For a minute, maybe two, no one said a word. Earl wondered when Mrs. French was going to fix the drinks. Right now, he really needed a belt. He glanced at her, but she showed no signs of getting up from her chair. Damn, Earl thought, he surely could have used a shot.

A heavy truck rumbled down the street. In another room a clock ticked. Then a jaybird started up and kept on until Earl thought he was going to scream. Everyone kept glancing at the others, then looking away. It was like a silent comedy out of the 20's, only there were no words on the screen, and no organ was accompanying, and no one was laughing.

Finally, Mr. French cleared his throat. "Well, I guess we all know why we are here. Don't we, Earl?"

"Suppose so."

"Not that there's anything good about any of this…"

"Bill."

"All right, Sue, all right. I'll try and refrain from commenting. But we're going to have to talk and we won't get very far if we keep interrupting each other." He turned his head and gave his wife one of his mayoral looks. As far as Earl could tell, she didn't seem particularly bothered. Kathy had begun to file her nails. The jay started up again.

Mr. French cleared his throat again. It sounded like he had some sort of lung disease. Earl closed his eyes. His life was like a nightmare. If only it were. At least then he'd eventually wake up.

"Now, as I was saying, we are all going to have to try and make lemonade out of this batch of lousy, rotten lemons. Isn't that right, Earl?"

"Guess so."

"What do you mean you guess so? Didn't Chief Evans talk to you?"

Earl closed his eyes until they were barely slit open. He could hardly stand to look at the mayor. What he really wanted to do was punch the old windbag. "I'm here, aren't I?"

"Ha. So far all you've done is eat and sit there beside my daughter with your eyes closed. We need to talk, I tell you."

"So talk."

He might be in a bad way, but he wasn't going to take crap off an old windbag like Bill French. Earl opened his eyes wider and sat up straighter. He could feel Kathy leaning against him. Heat radiated from her body. A pulse in Earl's right temple started to throb. The jay finally went quiet.

"There's no need to cop an attitude." Mr. French paused, then laughed. It wasn't much of a laugh, Earl thought, more of a snort, to his ear. Earl found himself liking the man less every minute, something he wouldn't have believed was possible.

"Oh, that was a good one. That's rich. Did you hear that, Sue, I just accused a cop of copping an attitude. Did you hear that, Kathy?"

"Calm down, Daddy, it's okay."

"Of course it's okay. Actually, it's more than okay. It's

damn funny, if I do say so myself."

Mr. French paused and cocked his head to one side, putting Earl in mind of a slightly jaded cockatoo.

"Don't you think it's funny, Earl? Me accusing you, of all people, of copping an attitude."

"Yeah, I think it's a real side-splitter. Now, can we get on with this talk you been yammering about all afternoon. For someone who's wanting to have a talk you sure are taking the long way around."

"Well, Officer, guess I should call you Earl, shouldn't I? Well, Earl, let's do get right down to the point. We all know the situation here, so I don't think we need to rehash the gory details or spell everything out. Agree? Okay. Then let's get right to the guts of the situation. Are you going to do the honorable thing? Or what?"

Earl sucked in air, held it, let it out slowly. As the air seeped out of his lungs it felt like it carried something else with it – a part of him, a very vital part of him. He couldn't put the feeling into words, but it was as though he was suddenly aware that nothing new or fun or exciting or good was ever going to happen in his life again. Somewhere between drawing in that breath and letting it out, he had grown old.

Earl licked his lips. God, how he wanted a drink, or two, right now. But drinking was what had gotten him into this mess, and he couldn't see how it would get him out.

Best he could see, there was no way out. Oh, he could walk out the door and down the driveway, get into his truck, and start driving. But where would that get him? The law did indeed have a long arm. No, actually what it had were long tentacles, like an octopus. That's what the law was – a giant octopus, and it would find him wherever he went and squeeze the holy shit out of him.

No doubt about that. Chief Evans had friends all over the

country. Earl wished he had a friend. Just one.

He rubbed at his face and then thrust it forward and gave them all a good hard look. Time to say what he had to say.

"This is a helluva mess we're in here. Now, I know a lot of it is my fault, but not all of it, and I don't see why I have to take the fall."

"But, Earl, I thought you loved me," Kathy wailed, burying her face in her hands.

Earl pushed the palms of his hands toward the others. Mr. French was half out of his chair and Mrs. French's eyes were damp. "Now hold on one minute. I didn't say I was skipping town. In fact, it might be better for me to stick around and head off any trouble that might come up."

"What the hell are you talking about, son? You aren't making a lick of sense."

"Just hear me out, Bill. What I'm saying is that, instead of me leaving town, it would be better for Kathy to go away. Just for a little while, see?"

"You've gone loco, Earl. Why in the name of all that's good and holy would Kathy go away? She needs her family with her at all times, but especially now."

"Yeah, but if she goes away, say to visit an aunt, why then no one ever has to know."

"But what about the baby?" Mrs. French whispered. "What about my grandchild?"

"Well…" Earl smiled and shrugged, trying to look innocent.

Mr. French leaned forward. His face had gone hard and ugly. "Earl Turner, you're not talking about what I think you're talking about, are you?"

"No, Bill, no, not that." Mrs. French began to sob, almost silently, her body convulsing.

"Don't cry, Mommy," Kathy whimpered and then she began to cry, too, softly at first, then louder with each sob.

Earl grimaced. His guts had started to churn again. "Come on, now, I'm not talking about anything in particular. I mean some real nice, well-off couple might be wanting a baby. There are ways. There are agencies."

Mr. French pushed up out of his chair. His hands formed fists. He stepped across the room and stood towering over Earl, his entire body trembling like low voltage electrical current was running through it.

"There will be no goddamn trips out of town, Earl, and no adoption, and no anything else except a walk down the aisle. Do you hear me?"

"Yeah, I hear you."

"Good, and if you don't I'll call Chief Evans and let him explain it to you again, real damn clear this time. You understand?"

Earl could feel the sides of his neck starting to flush. He wanted to punch Mayor French right in his fat gut. He jammed his hands deep in his pockets and made himself count to five.

"All right, I hear you. I was only suggesting an alternative that just might be better for all of us. But if you guys don't even want to discuss all our options, so be it. Only don't blame me, and for damn sure don't stand over me. I can't take anybody standing over me. It pisses me off, big time, and I won't be responsible for what I do."

Earl could sense his whole body vibrating, like it was a bomb getting ready to detonate. His brain felt hot and fluid, like cells were melting. He wanted to hit somebody or something really hard, over and over and over. Just like he had that Mexican.

His legs tightened and thrust him up from the settee. He

had no conscious control over them. They might has well have belonged to another man. Mr. French retreated a step, but their faces were still very close. Earl could feel the man's eyes on him. Little blue, icy, piggy eyes. Earl curled his fingers into fists.

Slowly, faintly at first, but then more insistently, a throbbing sound began to penetrate his consciousness. For a moment he couldn't place it. Then he recognized it and he felt his stomach turn over and his brain begin to cool.

The sound was the hoarse, wrenching sobs of a woman. Kathy was crying. Earl made a face and turned to her.

"Kathy, don't cry."

"You don't love me, Earl Turner. You lied to me. Nobody loves me, not really. I know that. Plus, I know I'm not real smart, but I know that much anyway."

"Now, Kathy."

"No, don't touch me. You got what you wanted. You only wanted me for one thing and you got it. Now go away. Go away. Go away and leave me alone."

Earl shut his eyes as he let the last drop of anger seep out. He could sense the eyes of her parents on him.

Mr. French was mumbling and Mrs. French was crying.

Earl wanted to scream.

He made himself open his eyes and turn slowly. He pushed at the air between him and the older couple with his open hands. "Go away, please. Leave us alone. Just for a little while."

Mr. French's face was twisted with emotion. Hatred, Earl figured, flavored heavily with anger.

"You are a real son-of-a-bitch, Turner."

"Yeah, I know it, but leave us alone. Let us talk for a moment in private, please."

"You better not hurt her anymore. If you do, I promise I'll

make you pay."

"Please," Earl said, struggling to keep his voice calm. "Five minutes. Give us five lousy minutes. I won't hurt her anymore, I swear."

He turned to Kathy's mother. "Mrs. French, you know how life can be at times? Give me a few minutes alone with Kathy, okay. I'll get things straightened out, I promise."

She lifted her face. Tears were running down her cheeks. Her eyes were red and watery. In that moment she reminded Earl of his mother. This was turning out to be a rat bastard of a day.

Mr. and Mrs. French simply stood there staring at him. Earl knew it was just his imagination, but his face felt hot where their glances landed. However, there was no question that their eyes were cold in their faces. Like round balls of ice, Earl thought.

After a moment he could hear a ticking inside his head, as though a metronome had suddenly formed inside his brain. He began counting. The count reached sixteen before Mr. French turned and nudged his wife.

"Come on, Sue, let's give them a few minutes." He put an arm around his wife's shoulders. "We'll be in the kitchen," he said with a quiet force.

Earl wasn't sure if he was supposed to be comforted or afraid. So he merely nodded.

The older couple turned then and started out of the room. They trudged slowly, as though they were on their way to a funeral. Earl eased down on the settee.

Kathy had scooted to the far edge of the settee. Earl stretched out a hand and started rubbing her back. He wanted to comfort her, but the right words wouldn't form in his brain. His mouth felt full of cotton and he wished he had a glass of water. Whiskey would also do nicely. He licked his lips and rubbed her back. Her muscles felt tight and stiff as though they were calcifying into bone. As he rubbed, he felt them gradually loosen.

"Don't cry, Kathy. It'll be all right."

She shook her head wildly, like a child. Her blonde hair swung back and forth, reminding Earl of wheat blowing before a storm.

"No it won't. You don't love me."

"Sure I do," Earl said, though the words were like small stones against his teeth.

"No you don't. You want to send me away."

"No I don't, not really. I was just saying that."

He swallowed, struggling to choke the lies down. "I just wanted everybody to be sure that they felt we were doing the best thing. Explore all the alternatives, you understand?"

Kathy didn't say anything. She only sobbed harder, her back rising and falling, the sobs crashing and retreating in rhythmic waves. Earl rubbed in slow, smooth circles, half-listening to the sobbing sounds, trying to figure out what to say that would make a difference.

Words had never been his long suit. Part of him simply wanted to say to hell with it all and get in his truck and start rolling. If he'd been ten, even five years, younger, he might very well have done that. Of course giving into emotions like that usually got him in trouble – like when he'd pounded on that Mexican.

Earl knew he would never say the words, but he recognized that even a Mex deserved something more than a beating. Besides, he wasn't a kid anymore and his parents needed him more every day, which meant he needed to stay close and stay on the job, and, therefore, he was – in every way he could see – in one bastard of a bind.

So he sat very still, only rubbing Kathy's back and trying

to come up with at least a few of the right words. He sensed his mind drifting, floating out of the room and down the drive, floating on and on, drifting on some unseen wind like a wayward cloud.

♦ ♦

A sudden quietness jerked Earl back into the room. Kathy's sobs had ceased and she had gone so still she looked somewhat like a statue or a mime.

"Kathy," Earl whispered.

She didn't speak. She didn't move. Earl had to look closely to determine that she was breathing.

"Kathy," he said again, his voice a few decibels louder.

She sniffed and shifted her position a few degrees, pressing her face against the settee.

"Kathy, I'm real sorry for making you so upset. Never meant to hurt your feelings. Now, I know you being in the family way, so to speak, why your nerves are surely more on edge than normal, so why don't we just put this afternoon behind us."

"For real?" she mumbled into the fabric of the settee.

Earl took a deep breath, then slowly let it out. Well, he supposed, like the condemned man of legend he'd eaten a hearty meal. "For real," he said, the words bitter and oily against his tongue.

She lifted her head, turning it just enough to let Earl see twin rows of tear tracks. He felt lower than a snake's belly, but he couldn't undo what had happened. For a girl that wasn't the brightest bulb in the pack, she sure knew how to play on his emotions.

"Are we still going to get married and have our baby, Earl? Hunh? Are we?"

"Sure," he said. "Sure we are."

A big smile spread across Kathy's face and before he could set himself she had twisted around and wrapped both arms behind his neck. They were wrapped so tightly he had trouble catching his breath.

"Oh, Earl, honey, I'm so happy. Let's go tell Mommy and Daddy." She pressed her lips against his cheek and then did it again, and again, and again. She was giggling. Earl, however, felt like crying. For a man about to get married, he sure wasn't looking forward to it. For the five hundredth time he asked himself why in the hell?

Damn, damn, damn, but I'm sure in one godawful bind now, he said to himself.

Even though he'd lived it, he didn't see how one man, who really wasn't a bad guy, could get himself in such a deep shithole. His life was over. Well, at least the life he knew. Actually, giving up some of it – the lonesome nights, the boredom, that sort of thing wouldn't be so bad.

In the end, he supposed, it was giving up his dreams that hurt. They might have been foolish, out-of-date, unrealistic dreams, but they were his dreams. And a man had to have dreams, or where the hell was he?

Now Earl knew the answer to that question. He was in a damn bad jam – that's where he was. He put a sickly grin on his face, stood, then started walking toward the door. Halfway there, he realized he was holding Kathy's hand.

The jay started back up and Earl paused for a second and listened. That stupid bird chattering was about the last sound of freedom he'd ever hear. He knew that. Just like he knew where a man was without any dream of his own.

Where was he?

Why, he was behind the eight ball. Yep, directly behind the damn eight ball.

Earl closed his eyes and listened to the jaybird while his bride-to-be squeezed his hand. Yes sir, he'd gotten himself into one crazy mess, one with no way out. Well, at least he was alive and not behind bars. Between the way he hammered that Mexican and what he'd done with Kathy he could have been looking at a lifetime behind bars. He'd have to learn to be grateful for small favors.

Earl shook his head. It felt strange to admit it, but he was sorry for beating on that Mex so long and hard. He was also sorry for not being a better son – his mom and dad deserved better. Well, that was something he'd sure tend to the first chance he got.

Most of his issues had been caused by anger coming out, anger at the world, his life, himself. Well, he'd have to learn to control his anger. He'd be glad to admit some lessons sure came a helluva lot harder than others.

Down the hallway, the clock struck seven. The tones sounded like the voice of doom to Earl. He took one more deep breath and squeezed Kathy's hand. The gallows stood at the end the hallway.

Images from a black and white movie flickered across his mind. It was a film about the French Foreign Legion and the old Legionnaire sergeant was speaking. For a moment, Earl couldn't make out the words. Then he heard them clear. "March or die, march or die."

He smiled then, a little for himself, and a little for all his celluloid heroes, and, finally, a little for his bride-to-be. Yep, he'd be taking a loss by giving up a way of life he'd known for all his adult life, but at least he'd finally belong to someone, someone different, but then wasn't everybody different in their own way.

Earl straightened up, sucked in his gut, stuck his chin out and pretended he was Gary Cooper in the French Foreign

Legion. He linked arms with Kathy and they started marching down the hall toward the kitchen, toward their future. As they marched, Earl whistled softly. Halfway there, he realized he was whistling the marching tune that the prisoners whistled in *Bridge on the River Kwai.*

Of Two Lives

On The Lower Golan

Howard R. Wolf

Note from Howard R. Wolf: For pronunciation assistance and definitions of Yiddish words, I suggest Leo Rosten's The Joys Of Yiddish.

LUDWIG FRIED, no Gerhardus Mercator but an explorer of inner *and* outer landscapes, slumped in his chair in the El Al lounge at JFK airport, waiting to board his night flight to Tel Aviv a few hours before the winter solstice – his favorite time of the year, with winter darkness yielding to lengthening days. Mercifully, skies were clear. If he was lucky, not likely given his history, but possible, he might have a smooth trip. Light turbulence, at a minimum, was his middle initial.

Through the floor to ceiling windows, he could see the spans of the old TWA terminal, emblem of 1950's optimism and postwar panache, arcing towards puffy white clouds that drifted across a full moon. They looked to him like wisps of Ben-Gurion's hair as Ludwig waited in a somewhat dreamy state two hours before departure.

If he couldn't claim to be floating down the stream of consciousness between the banks of Yin and Yang, he was paddling his internal canoe between the shores of Column A and Column B of Broadway's vanished House of Chan, a legacy of his childhood, the one place his father had acted like the head of a "family," a word his pop never had used.

The House of Chan had become for his father and his cronies in the garment business something like Plymouth Rock,
a place of Thanksgiving for the bounty of the New World:
egg foo yung replacing turkey at the banquet table and
wonton soup serving as a mini-Provincetown Bay, especially if you sailed a mini-bamboo umbrella from one side of
the bowl to the other.

It was easier for Ludwig to understand the family of man
than his own. His father had been too obsessed with being
bankrupt to think about anything else. He had been bankrupt
so often, poor guy, it might have been said that he was "in"
bankruptcy as other fathers, in Ludwig's neighborhood and
social world, were "in" furs, diamonds, and zippers. His father, born on the Lower East Side just after the turn of the
century, a virtual immigrant, had made his way through the
canyons of the garment center to the upper reaches of Washington Heights.

The Manhattan of his childhood was gone, of course, as
was TWA, but they lingered in dreams – sometimes his father even spoke to him in the middle of the night, as did his
father's father, Jacob, in broken Yiddish or splintered English. Just about everything had two sides, and sometimes the
sides had sides. String Theory might not be such a crazy idea
after all. Here he was about to make a trip that he both did
and didn't want to make, and he could make a list of posi-
tives and negatives on both sides of the equation during the
night-flight and send them to M.I.T. for analysis.

His daughter Marion might be doing better – he wasn't
sure. Ludwig had lost his ball-bearings, if not his balls, for a
while in the 1960's, clunking along on the highway of free
love, for which he paid tolls later, and so he hadn't been able
to give his daughter a reliable trip-tick. It was hard to make
up for divorce and separation.

It would be difficult for her to find her way, her road-map. He hoped to discover on this trip if she had made a solid marriage after a decade when she seemed often enough to be lost. "Solid" might be just as important as "good," given the turbulence of the past. One didn't have to be airborne to hit an air-pocket.

He would draw up a list during what he knew would be a sleepless night over the Atlantic, but he was pretty sure he wouldn't be able to resolve the contradictions, the differences between his daughter's new life and his old one: her rejection of his academic complexities and psychological ambivalences – "Mental *mishegas*, Dad" – for what she took to be the firm foundation of a simpler life and a healthier one for her children.

She didn't see that her quest for simplicity had complicated his life, but she had a right to choose *her* life. She trusted him, without thinking about it, to accept her choices. He hoped he could find a saving remnant of America, the one they had shared together, in her New Jerusalem.

At the same time, he wasn't sure the American remnant was worth saving. If Hannity and the Gang of Foxes were the new media version of Mt. Rushmore, and if Kim Kardashian had replaced the Venus de Milo as an icon of beauty, well, *dash* it all (he chortled to himself), he didn't think the country could fulfill its foundational promises any more. Tom Paine was probably throwing up somewhere in the beyond.

And they were just Talking Heads. They weren't sending people to secret prisons to be tortured. Ludwig preferred Glenn Miller's rendition of "Moonlight Serenade" to the dark world of the C.I.A. and Trump's nightmare vision of a "deep State."

Maybe the Promised Land, despite many broken promises and shattered bodies, to say nothing of psyches, did make more sense. He shouldn't be too pessimistic. Sir Arthur Balfour himself had said that "Man will go down into the pit, and all his thoughts will perish," and yet he had come up in 1917 with the crucial Declaration. The hope of a homeland for the Jews had arisen from the ashes of his personal despair.

Something similar had happened to Marion. Out of a confused decade when she had been lost and he thought he had lost her, she had emerged, a single mother, with a vision of a new future for herself and her son. In a sense, having a son had saved her – making a good life for him. Still, he didn't know how he would react when he first saw Marion and her family, especially the first born son, in their new home at the edge of the moshav overlooking the Kinneret – "Just looking at it makes me feel whole, Dad, wait till you see it from here."

A quick look around the departure lounge made the point about life's reversible surfaces like the raincoats his father had manufactured in Newark and sold in the showroom on West 37th Street: toddlers clung to their mothers who sat next to strangers with whom they chatted, becoming fast friends before take-off, perhaps never to talk again, only to wave goodbye in Tel Aviv, waiting to clear Customs. Airport lounges bred intimacies more intense than French affairs, but, unlike Shalimar, didn't leave a scent.

Ludwig had lived many versions of a double life, a Chagall-like rendering of post-World War II Jewish American possibilities of existence and identity. His life had been somewhat complicated and semi-comic – the latter, perhaps, because he hadn't been as gifted as Chagall. Compared to the proprietor of Kurtzman's Candy Store, Kurtzman (who else?), in his old Manhattan neighborhood of Washington Heights, he had achieved a *nosh* of achievement. But no smorgasbord.

If Kafka had needed an axe to "break up the frozen sea within us," Ludwig had knocked icicles off eaves of his psyche – he wasn't sure about the soul – with a garden tool in the dead of winter in the silence of a Western New York night.

And he could count on having icicles as long as cathedral size organ pipes so long as he lived on the edge of Lake Erie where the ice-booms on the Niagara River weren't removed until late spring. But icicles weren't meat-hooks on which Nazi victims were hanged.

Ludwig, a transplanted New Yorker, was not the original Ludwig Fried. His great uncle, of Zbecno, Czechoslovakia was killed...murdered...gassed...incinerated...in Terezin September 3, 1942.

Against his great uncle's "suffering" (was there one word?), Ludwig Fried's anguish – an adjunct lecturer and minor writer in an upstate university where most students were more interested in Facebook than The Book of Knowledge – was petty, trivial, and obscure. But it was, after all, *his* anguish; and each person was entitled to treasure his own chopped *tsuris*.

The original Ludwig Fried's fate came to define the doubleness of Ludwig's life when he learned late, at his mother's ninetieth birthday party, about the life and death of his late-great uncle from a cousin, once removed, whom he never had met before.

Uncle Ludwig, may he rest in peace, unlikely, now lay in Ludwig's mind in the center of a historical panorama in which Ludwig only could play somewhat guiltily an indirect and minor role. He could try to salvage the memory of his incinerated uncle, to mourn the six million, but nothing else.

This revelation had displaced and marginalized other two-sided dimensions of his life. This terrible fact had become the North Star of his consciousness. Its tragic brightness cast shadows across the other ambivalences of his life. He had lived in the Diaspora of Western New York for many decades, but the main coordinates of his life were elsewhere: Lauderhill, Florida, mother; father buried beneath a metal plaque two streets north of Commercial Boulevard – turn left at The Pastrami Club, right at Vegas Nights; Estoril, Portugal, brother; Ramat HaGolan, Israel, daughter; Ithaca, lost love; Manhattan, his lost youth.

Even Western New York, aka "Niagara Frontier," was elsewhere, its Native American roots uprooted, its fabled past only a fable now. Onguiaahra and Iroquois League of Six Nations merely names, remembered only, like so much else, by Google. Freud now might as well have said, "Where there was Id, let there be Google." Google had become for the early twenty-first century what the Dynamo had been for Henry Adams at the 1900 Great Exposition in Chicago – an invisible force as powerful as the virgin in the Middle Ages.

He knew when every bush on his small plot of land would flower in the spring, but the larger plot of life and its flowering or blight had yet to reveal itself. As much as Ludwig loved to tend his garden, an irregular Voltaire, as much as he mulched his evergreens, he knew that his psyche had roots in many faraway places. He seemed unable to cultivate one garden.

If he had a native soil, it was in some god-forsaken village in Lithuania whose name he never had known and which now was part of Poland, Russia, or Kaliningrad. He had grown up in a world where important place-names often were mispronounced so he couldn't find them on any map.

The Old World was a mythic place without a longitude or latitude. More of an attitude.

He had tried for many years without success to find out, over a bowl of borscht, where dollops of sour cream drifted like pilgrim boats on the Kinneret, from his Yiddish speaking paternal grandfather just where the family had come from; but his grandfather's English was thicker than the borscht, especially at Harris's Dairy Bar on Upper Broadway where they met once a year, so Ludwig never had found out if his grandfather even knew where he was from or if his *shtetl* had a name.

Besides, Jacob, at his age, was more interested in the borscht than the past. And there might be a memory problem; he didn't want to press Jacob on this point. His grandfather had wrestled with enough problems in his life, peddler in the New World, a dealer in end-pieces, rags, and remnants. His grandfather's rags had given way to his father's 7th Avenue *shmattes* which, in turn, had made possible the warp and woof of Ludwig's life, more warp than woof, Brooks Brothers with, sometimes at a bar mitzvah or on the one day he pretended to be observant, Yom Kippur, a yarmulke set at a rakish angle like a Broadway sharpie.

"Questions, questions…who cares about the past?"

Ludwig was of many places, so what was the point of looking for a center of gravity? It was no use looking for a GPS when it came to identity if you were a third generation American Jew who lived in a world of fragmented languages he didn't understand and fragments of stories that hadn't yet made up a coherent narrative.

He lived in a world of echoes of loss and belonging, of patches, swatches and unintelligible murmurs, never sure if he could come up with a real tune that he could hum or a whole cloth that he could drape over his shoulders like a tallith.

There had been times when he hadn't been able to take a step forward or backward, left or right, when ambivalence had wrapped him in a mental strait-jacket. Then he would think about people who were something like really mad, and he would take a baby-step forward, pretending that he was playing Simple Simon.

He was a person of many places, of many sides. Just like the crisscrossed runways and the arrival-departure flight paths that he could see beyond the broad-brimmed hats of some Orthodox Jews who sat in the lounge in front of him.

Who was and who wasn't a rabbi still was a mystery to him, but it didn't matter – they all were absolutely certain about motives and obligations that still bewildered him and that he assumed always would be baffling. For them, there were 613 *mitzvot*; for him, there might be 612, 614, or none.

The runway lights sparkled in the chill winter air, appropriate for the holidays' seasons and his grandson's sixteenth birthday in two weeks: L22 looked like Hanukkah; R23 looked like Christmas. Soon the Hindus, Baha'is, and Moslems would be asking Mayor Bloomberg for *their* runways. Why not? This was New York in the age of multi-culturalism.

His daughter had planned a festive celebration for his arrival on an open field at the edge of Moshav Giv'at Yo'av overlooking the Kinneret at an elevation of 1,500 feet. There would be a blue and white tent, barbeque grills, and an Israel Defense Force (IDF) youth chorus. It might be cold, but it would be thrilling to see the lights of Tiberias from the hill on which she lived draped across the landscape like a multi-tiered necklace. But the lights gave way to shadows in his mind, heart, soul, psyche, nervous system – all the components, whatever they were (who really knew?).

He didn't want to think of the time in two years when David would wear an IDF uniform. He wanted to preserve the image of the little boy he so had adored who would spin on his head, feet on the slanted pine wood ceiling, before going to sleep in the years when David's mother had brought him home in the aftermath of a turbulent first marriage. Her turbulence had recreated, in different terms, the wind-shear drop of his marriage, *her* parents'. Being broken was a family tradition, it seemed.

The thought of David as a tank commander or helicopter pilot – the boy had leadership abilities and was good with his hands – brought back memories of the summer war of 2006.

He didn't want to think about David garrisoned at a post somewhere at the base of Mt. Hermon or at a dangerous checkpoint on the West Bank. He wasn't sure he could face the boy, now a young man, without breaking and revealing his anxiety. And that was something he never wanted the boy to see. The boy held his grandfather inside him as a source of strength, and Ludwig couldn't let David see that he was vulnerable. He would leave before that ever would happen.

He recalled his daughter's first summer in Israel, her near-poverty, her inability without his help to live in a style to which she was accustomed – somewhere between Wal-Mart and Lord & Taylor. He had raised her, after all, to become something like an enlightened version of Barbara Walters, and now she was turning into a version of Sophie Tucker. Not my "Yiddisha Momma" exactly, but a throwback, like a swatch of gabardine, the fabric which, when it became passé in 1949, had put his father out of business.

He knew that she probably would have given up on a life in Israel without his help, and he had been tempted, lacking a serious partner – no therapist, not even Woody Allen's, had been able to solve this problem for him – to let her fail so she would come back to America. That would be selfish and weak, of course, but why should he be different from other minor league narcissists?

Why had he always resisted the most obvious forms of security and comfort? A warm body in the night was enough to keep most couples together. He had chosen to go it alone most of the time in lieu of…he didn't know what. Country clubs, congregations, and gyms were all the togetherness that most people needed. He, big-shot, had chosen to take a different path. Not the road not taken, but the road where his failure to make conventional choices had let him off.

So, sitting at the water's edge of the Kinneret at Kibbutz En Gev, strategic outpost in the 1948 war, he had decided to help them. He had taken her and David to the kibbutz's Holiday Village for a night to think through her decision, and he had seen how alive and content she looked watching her son splash around in the gleaming white-caps that whipped up in the mid-afternoon and rippled across the lake from west to east.

Ludwig knew that it meant a great deal for her to see her son play in this ancient lake, a lake whose history might make up for some of the riptides in her own life and her son's – just as he had understood, without ever discussing it with her, her desire to put the boy in a Hebrew day school a few years earlier where a sense of tradition might make up somehow for the lack of a live-in father.

Ludwig knew, somehow, more than she herself may have known, she was trying to make up for a failure of her personal history by immersing her son in a deeper history. He decided then – looking at her looking at her child, running into the waves and flapping his arms as if to fly over them –

to help her make Aliyah. He couldn't afford it, but, big deal!; he would refinance his house. Life might be short, but mortgages were long. Primary commitments were one thing, sub-prime another. Maybe he could get MGM to change their motto.

In the spur of the moment, he had pledged to help her stay in Israel even if it meant that he would have to teach freshman composition for a few years longer than he ever planned to. It wasn't a fate worse than death, even if the placing of an exclamation point had become an emotional issue for many students in the fast-approaching post-print era, Romanticism's last punctuation mark.

"Oh, Daddy! Will you really help me stay?" she just about shouted, hugging him.

"Yes, Marion, I will, what else is a father for?"

"Well, there are credit cards, just kidding."

In imagining her and the boy now, he felt that he was with them, but he was alone as usual, a paradox in the crowded and noisy lounge where families shared food, babies slept in their mother's arms, and men in frock coats pointed out passages in a Midrash, Mishneh Torah, and the Talmud. They talked loudly in varieties of English, Hebrew, and Yiddish, pointing and touching the stiff brims of their hats for emphasis.

Ludwig's bar mitzvah, ages ago, had left him somewhat traumatized by these ancient texts he couldn't understand. More interested as a high school student in dating girls from the East Side than the Near East, he had tried to walk away from all incomprehensible mysteries, but they had returned somehow. It never had occurred to him that his bar mitzvah with its haul of war bonds, gold pens, and tie-clasps would have staying power like Al Singer, "the Bronx Beauty," his father's buddy, who had stayed on his feet two rounds in

1931 after he had lost vision in one eye, poor guy.

Only one thing was clear: he was an outsider to all this koan-like biblical talk. No Jack Kerouac or Alan Ginsburg, he had been quietly subversive nonetheless and remained so, at least here, in this lounge, at this time. But it would be different, at least for a while, despite all the difficulties, once he got to Israel and saw his daughter and her family. She had married a man who was attached to the good earth, cultivated olives and pomegranates, and drove a tractor. Ludwig didn't have to worry, so far, about getting wrapped up in *tefillin*.

But he would have to come to terms with her life in a new land and what would be in time, if not already, David's homeland, even as western New York might linger in memory or dreams as a lost origin. Old and new had flip-flopped. David might become a new man in an old land; Ludwig, not even a Reform Jew, had to face a new set of realities at an age when most men had sunk their last putt or puttered in a garden.

"El Al Flight 18 will be boarding in ten minutes, please have your boarding passes ready. We apologize for the delay."

Ludwig looked around him carefully, really for the first time. So these were the people with whom his fate would be sealed for the next ten or eleven hours, depending on the weather and the jet-stream. If he was lucky, not his MO, the seat next to his would be empty so he could fidget and toss without disturbing anyone, but this was unlikely just after Hanukkah with families and friends returning from New York to Israel.

As luck would have it, he was sitting next to a portly rabbi with a beard so long and full that it would probably tickle his ears in the middle of the night like a Turkish barber and wake him up if he could manage to fall asleep for an hour or so. He was one of those people who believed that he had to stay awake to keep the plane in the air and who, if he flushed the toilet in flight, would blow off an engine.

So he would spend most of the night in a semi-conscious state, squeezing his bladder until it was so painful that he had to risk a mid-air disaster. And when he pushed the flush button, he would come as close to prayer as he was capable of: not belief, but magic, if the distinction could be made.

As the plane taxied down the tarmac, he introduced himself to his seatmate. Nothing induced a sense of fellowship more than the first thrust of ascent when there would be no statistical possibility for another miracle on the Hudson if there was a mishap, not this time of year, not at night.

"Ludwig Fried," he nodded, mustering something like a smile in the direction of the dour rabbi. Well, maybe he was just a member of some Chasidic synagogue, Crown Heights, for instance. Or a follower of the Lubavitcher Rebbe, Rabbi Menachem M. Schneerson – "some say rebbe, some say rabbi, let's call the whole thing cloth," he was tempted to hum.

He was embarrassed he didn't know all the fine distinctions among Jewish American sects and persuasions, to say nothing of world Jewry, but the truth of his identity – assimilated, ambivalent, confused – was his excuse, and the truth was its own defense. If the Lubavitchers would accept the Emerson in his *pushke* – the one his mother had insisted he always should have at home in case a collector For Resettlement of Jewish Refugees from Cochin to the State of Israel should turn up – then he would struggle to accept the hidden depths in his holiness's spiritual pickle barrel.

119

The stern looking ultra-Orthodox someone, whom he didn't expect to yiddle on his verbal fiddle in response, looked at Ludwig, tipped the brim of his fedora, and held up a black-covered book that he clutched in his left hand.

"*The* book," he said.

"A good book," Ludwig replied.

"*Only* book," he glowered in response.

They weren't off to a good start, but they were off the ground, circling over Jamaica Bay, heading east over the coast of Long Island, lights twinkling faintly below in the Hamptons, maybe Sag Harbor, where he wished his daughter had settled instead of Israel, or so he wished in this moment. He hadn't wanted her to be a worshipper at the altars (or was it halters?) of Versace and Gucci, but he hadn't been immune to the allure of conventional success for her.

Ludwig felt a little sheepish about reading Philip Roth's *The Breast*, but he wasn't going to be intimidated. He wasn't going to hide his book. In fact, he held up the flesh-toned cover of the book, with its pink bull's-eye nipple, so the rabbi-rebbe-whatever could see it.

"*Nisht mit drek, kinder, nisht.*"

He hadn't been called "kinder" since he was a child, and he was tempted to agree up to a point with his disagreeable seatmate, but he wasn't going to cave in to blind Orthodoxy, especially when the old man – all the Orthodox looked old to him – lowered the brim of his fedora so as not to see the offending cover, as if it was a "money-shot" in a porn movie, which it was in a sense, but Ludwig was fighting for *his* own identity. He wasn't going to exchange it for anyone else's.

In defiance, Ludwig said, "But he's a Jew, Roth's an American Jew."

The old man belched, as if Ludwig was giving him a case of moral indigestion, and lowered the brim of his hat further, puffing up his beard, putting a hairy cloud between himself and Ludwig. Ludwig would get back at the son-of-a-vitcher somehow for making him feel guilty about who he was. The old man, who probably wasn't any older than Ludwig, looked like Martin Buber's unkempt cousin, and he arrogantly believed in only one "Thou."

His grandson hadn't shown any signs of becoming ultra-religious so far, but who knew what the future held? He did work after school polishing shofars in a small factory, and this work, in time, might turn the shape of his soul into a ram's horn. And when David went into the IDF, he might, when faced with danger, turn to prayer. Most men did and then there would be more distance between them.

But who was he to be so judgmental? As Hem had put it in "Snows of Kilimanjaro": "However you make your living is where your talent lies." If true, who was he? How had he made his living? Maybe he could figure some of it out before he left Israel this time. On a ridge overlooking the Kinneret, he might catch a glimpse of the circle of his life before he left. Just like him – he was leaving before he arrived.

Looking through the wisps of the observant man's beard at flecks of phosphorescent clouds, Ludwig wanted to believe that he would remain the boy's trusted authority, even as he knew that such a thought was selfish, vain, and foolish. This was especially true since he didn't believe in any ultimate authority beyond Wordsworth's "still sad music of humanity," and he wasn't sure what that was, though he sometimes thought he heard strains of it on certain summer evenings when the sound of a distant wind-chime and the fluttering of his smoke-bush seemed to be in harmony or when he listened to Paul Desmond play his dreamy, but disciplined, alto saxophone, "Take Five!"

The tracery of lights below was becoming fainter with

more areas of darkness between them. The plane was bank-ing northeast towards Boston and soon would be over the Maritimes. Then it would be a wing and a hope that no Ji-hadist was aboard the rest of the way. If he was lucky, he would be able to make some sense of his life through the night with intervals of sleep in between, unless the rabbi's wispy beard tickled his ear and kept him awake most of the time.

With luck, he would have some uninterrupted time to ex-amine his aloneness and isolation at an age and stage of life when most of the men he knew had made separate peaces, pre-nups, and funeral pre-plans. He had played emotional roulette with his emotional pistol, and there were still a few loaded chambers left.

He buried himself in *The Breast*: "Doctor, I want to fuck her! With my nipple!" He was dying to read this to the rabbi. He looked slyly at the reverent, if unpleasant, man who was poring over pages of his book with one hand and with the other tucking small rolled scrolls of parchment with Hebrew writing on them into the depth of his beard and then squeez-ing the end of his beard to make sure that the tubes stayed in place.

Although he never had looked inside a mezuzah, or even touched one reverentially as he entered or left his house, Ludwig knew that these oblongs contained the sacred words from Deuteronomy: "Hear, O Israel, the Lord our God, the Lord is one," the essential prayer of Judaism, an affirmation of monotheism that upset the pagan world and its gods and continues to upset those who would wish to project more stars and celebrities into the firmament.

His companion's behavior was peculiar, to say the least. If stowing scrolls in a scruffy beard was an ancient rite, an Essenic mystery, he was unaware of it. But it seemed to be

more of a neurotic tic or a small scam, possibly selling mezuzah scrolls on the cheap to five-star hotels, The King
David, maybe, or in shadowy recesses of the Western Wall.

But it might be something more sinister. Maybe he was a
Jihadist in disguise, an undercover agent carrying a message,
or blueprint for an IED, from a cell in New York to one in
the West Bank. This was doubtless a paranoid fantasy on
Ludwig's part, the product of an insoluble conflict to which
no one could find a solution, but still, he would keep an eye
on his quietly belligerent seatmate to make sure he didn't set
his beard on fire in a quest for martyrdom.

If his traveling companion ever fell into a deep sleep and
began to snore like a *chazzan*, Ludwig might try to pat him
down lightly to see if he was wired or rigged in some strange
way. It was unlikely that he had stowed some nitro in his
BVDs, but it wasn't impossible, given the fantasies of re-
venge that could become facts when it came to Israel; and
these *frum* types were given an E-Z pass as a rule when it
came to security. Their apparent piety was a perfect disguise.

Ludwig was embarrassed by these thoughts, to be sure.
He had been Bar Mitzvahed properly, if superficially, in a
Conservative synagogue, Ansche Chesed, West End Avenue
and 100th St., NYC (did it still exist?), not that he was aware
of the congregational distinctions at the time. It was only half
a century later at David's bar mitzvah that he had had a
glimpse of the meaning of the ritual, its pledged commitments.

And he still stood in awe, or sat in this case, of religious
men in frock coats whose white beards looked like cumulous
clouds behind which hid their invisible G-d. He still em-
ployed the hyphen in his thoughts, lest his late grandfather,
a kvetching kraken, emerge from his unconscious and smite
him like an Old Testament prophet.

How could he doubt the man's authenticity when he emitted the slight scent of an old pickle – a sign of ethnic identity, if ever there was one, especially for someone like Ludwig for whom a pickle lying atop or athwart a Sabrett's hot dog was a like a royal escutcheon, a coat of arms, no bar sinister, but: *A Pickle in the Middle with Mustard on Top.*

He was, after all, someone for whom a Manischewitz label of Sacramental Concord Grape Wine, "Wine Like Mother Used To Make," had the power virtually of the Torah itself on High Holy Days, when he wasn't being observant, to make his knees weak – as if to force him into a prayerful posture.

Against such a strong force of memory and gratuitous guilt, how could he not muster up some trust or put some sauerkraut on his misapplied quotient of mistrust? He remembered the frail Yeshiva student who had struggled and failed to teach him proper Hebrew so that it would not sound as if his pronunciation of the "khet" required a Heimlich maneuver. He remembered and felt guilty.

Memory and guilt were a powerful combination like horseradish on Rumanian pastrami – enough to give you heartburn, to make the mind think of ashes, not Fitzgerald's symbolic valley, but the real mortal residue, even the death-camps.

Now the learned man, his fedora brim tipped towards Ludwig, slept and snored in low cantorial rhythms and intonations, not unlike the hum of the Boeing 737 engines. Turbulence made most men believers, including Ludwig, even as cold skepticism returned when the plane touched down on the tarmac, so he wanted to believe that his companion's murmurings were helping to keep the plane aloft.

Every now and then, a number or word would waft through his devout neighbor's cloudy beard: 47...June...

76.... Was he counting *mitzvot* the way an ordinary man would count sheep or, if his unconscious was active and his personal censor also was asleep, flipping through dimly remembered pages of *Penthouse* centerfolds where cartoon size breasts replaced apples in the mind's Garden of Eden. Like everything else, at least for the likes of Ludwig, paradise was relative. Everything was relative, as he often said, except one's relatives, one of Ludwig's few absolute convictions.

Pious or not, Jew or Gentile, imam or rabbi, Pat Robertson or Updike, few men, or any, were immune to fantasies of what a former colleague had called "dreams of mammalian comfort." "In sleep, one didn't have to be an eager beaver to seek refuge in the cave of Venus or a hungry infant to crave a nipple. There were ancient needs that made all men bedfellows, if not bosom buddies, or buddies of bosoms."

One didn't have to be a Freudian or a neuroscientist to know that there was something like an "id" or "old brain" that tickled one's fancy on Mediterranean evenings when the scent of mangoes was in the air or when a *kibbutznik* ran bare-breasted through a date palm grove seeking to recover some of the lingering free love spirit of the pioneer era in Israel in the 1960's. Those days were a dream, but dreams were powerful.

He wondered what his slumbering neighbor would do if placed in the front row of the Folies Bergère. Would he daven or say a *barukh* – thanking God that he got to Paris before he died?

Would the imperatives of the Torah hold fast when faced with breasts so shapely that they might be mistaken for the sweetest and roundest of brioches in the darkness of the cabaret, or navel oranges in the original groves of Micanopy,

Florida, where Moses Levy, a Moroccan Jew and dreamer, had bought 50,000 acres for development?

Ludwig was tempted to tug just a little on the old man's wispy beard to ask him what he thought of Josephine Baker or, if that was out of his Brooklyn neighborhood, Gypsy Rose Lee. *Playboy* could be a fallback position. After all, everyone went to a dentist's office or, if they didn't have insurance, to a barber shop.

Even observant men needed haircuts, but, maybe not, maybe just a little snip now and then to make sure their locks didn't get entangled in the *tefillin*. But this was not the time and these were not the days to tug on anyone's beard in a plane. It would be all too easy for a nudnick to be mistaken for a terrorist. And how would his word stand up against a man of black cloth on an El Al flight to Tel Aviv?

Better to think of Bridget Bardot and let it go at that. Poor Bridget, she might be asking for forgiveness in some church on the Riviera for all the masturbatory fantasies she had inspired, including Ludwig's. God knows, he, no Catholic, had flogged the bishop himself more than a few times on summer nights in Washington Heights when the lights on the cables of the GW Bridge had twinkled messages of travel. He had imagined then that one day he and Bridget might pulsate to the rhythms of "You're the Top," she, topless, and he, bottomless, on a private beach in Cannes.

But these reveries weren't teaching him anything about himself, and he wasn't getting anywhere, though the plane was, at least so far. Now was the moment to make up a list of his life's opposing forces. There had been doubleness and thus confusion from the beginning from his life: conceived in the Bronx, exodus to Manhattan, his first Diaspora.

In times like this, he regretted that he hadn't studied philosophy instead of literature as an undergraduate. In fact, he had tried, but his P's reversed themselves and turned into Q's. He had been good, finally, at least better, at dotting his i's. It always had been embarrassing when his roommate from Kansas, as naïve then as a young person could be, told Ludwig what he, Ludwig, *really was thinking*, when he, Westy, had a few deep insights about his New York Jewish classmate. Westy later discovered Wittgenstein and got hooked up with the daughter of a Talmudic scholar and spent summers schmoozing with psychoanalysts in Provincetown. Then there had been a real meeting of East and Midwest.

His seatmate was now deep into REM, doubtless counting herring as they swam upstream to return to their natal spawning grounds, snoring in harmony with the plane's big engines. Harmony was not Ludwig's thing. He was a divided man who stood on both sides of many gorges and ravines. He could make a list, starting with "born on the Grand Concourse, ascended to Washington Heights."

This in itself told the main story of his life – echoes of the old world, the swing of the new. He preferred Cole Porter and Billy Holiday to the typical warbling of most cantors, especially the lay ones who thought they sounded like Dean Martin on the Day of Atonement.

But there were moments when, if he found himself in an orthodox synagogue for some obligatory reason, the ancient sounds vibrated deep in his psyche, as if he had heard these sounds and rhythms in a previous life. No mystic, he wondered if music could be genetically encoded and transmitted from generation to generation. Maybe there was a cosmic meme-cee.

This basic division in his life had subdivisions like gated communities in Boca Raton and Palm Beach. Somehow, the equation had been reversed for his daughter, as if she had been born in Manhattan and raised in the Bronx, not that she had been born or raised in either borough. Born in Madison, Wisconsin, she had been raised in many places, but not New York, except for visits to grandparents. Maybe not having one point of origin was her problem, if she had a problem. He wasn't sure.

He thought he had raised his daughter to be chic and progressive, a regular City Honors girl. It had seemed inevitable, given the way that they had lived and where they had lived, separately and together, for vacations and longer periods: Mexico, Vermont, Berkeley, Greenwich Village, Buffalo, Florida, Hong Kong. But she had turned out to be retrogressive and *haimish*.

He had assumed that her early displacements and later movements would make her a glamour-puss with a deep longing to live in a place like Sag Harbor, where she would lounge on a deck with a high-ball and *The New Yorker*. And she had been on that trail for a while, but, then, out of the blue, or so it seemed, she had made *aliyah*!

Had she been running away, or had she found something? And had she found something for him as well? Was all his overseas travel – sleepless night on planes, indigestion, being imposed upon by an impossible faux rabbi who smelled like a Nathan's hot dog – going to add up to something important, or would it turn out to be another period of complications and confusion for both of them? Well, the proof would be in the *kugel* of her life.

He was getting groggy. He might not sleep deeply, but he could enter a somewhat numb zone. All he needed to do was to read something. That always worked in this Poe-like hypnologic state between consciousness and unconsciousness. For a nice Jewish boy, at any age, reading could act like a narcotic. He pulled out a copy of *Tel Aviv Today* from the seat pocket in front of him.

In an article on "The Origin of the Name of Tel Aviv," he read that "Theodore Herzl's *Alteneuland,* 'Old New Land,' had been translated into Hebrew in 1910 as 'Tel Aviv,' 'Hill of Spring'." Bingo, it seemed almost too ambivalent to be true. Here he was – semi-Ivy League, assimilated – going into an old land. His daughter, tired of the New World, had found motherhood and a kind of rebirth in a new old land.

Looking back, he could see that she had been preparing for something all along without either of them knowing it. She had written from college once that Eliot's line, "And the Jew squats on the window sill" was *shmutz*. He hadn't expected her to become a literary critic, but she was right on the money about this one. Burdened by rumination, he slumped to the side and fell asleep, nestled close to "the big Coney Island hot dog in the sky, mustard on the top and pickle in the middle," as he thought of his rumpled neighbor.

For the first time in his life, he heard music in his dreams, "Hatikvah." He didn't realize that his unconscious knew all the notes of the melody, a regular Tin Pan Back Alley. Fraulein Gretchen Baumeister, the eminent neuro-musicologist, with whom he had had a brief fling in Berlin, had told him that she heard "Kol Nidrei" sometimes in her dreams, but he had dismissed these claims as a form of post-Nazi era guilt and felt sorry for her.

But his hidden mind had been eavesdropping and was a better Jew than Ludwig himself, even as "it" was obviously part of Ludwig. The composer Samuel Cohen would have been proud of Ludwig while he slept, if not while he was awake. It had taken seventy years for the song to become the anthem of Israel, and it had taken Ludwig almost as many years to get to the troubled country himself. Israel wasn't "Ma Vlast" for Ludwig, but there was a deep connection for him and a connection to *the* tragedy. After all, the original

Ludwig was from Bohemia, not Greenwich Village.

He leaned back on the chaise lounge in his dream and tapped his finger on the wide brim of the rabbi's fedora in time to the music. But it wasn't a dream. He had awakened as the 737 banked towards Tel Aviv coastline, and he could see palm trees on the edges of the runways in the distance. For a moment he thought he was in Miami Beach, or perhaps revisiting it in the 1940's of his dream life, but, no, it was real music, and much to his surprise he felt some moisture in the corner of his eyes.

He didn't want his grumpy flight mate to think that he had been moved by the sight of Israel, and it was possible that he had been stirred by the image of what he had taken to be Miami Beach, so he lowered his face and pressed a now crumpled page of Roth's book against his face.

Dry-eyed, he glanced at the snoring *shnorrer*, who seemed to be davening in his sleep and occasionally checking his beard to make sure all the scrolls were deeply embedded and hidden. Maybe he wasn't a *shnorrer* after all, maybe he just had a deep need to keep the sacred texts as close to his body as possible.

It was a preternaturally blue day, unusual for this time of year, except for a few tallish-white puffy clouds. As the wheels touched the tarmac, the would-be or could-be smuggler leaned close and whispered, "Get any titty in your sleep, boychik?"

It wasn't clear from the expression on his face if this was an interested inquiry or an accusation. For all Ludwig knew, this maybe-imposture might be a googler of Jewish porn websites, if there were any. Once Ludwig had googled "Jewish Porn" and *The Norton Anthology of Jewish Literature* had come up. If the creep knew about nookie, anything might be possible.

"Well, boychik, it's been an experience, but don't blow on my cover," his nighttime companion said, as he touched his Bible to his fedora, setting it at a rakish angle, and then pushed in the tips of those mysterious scrolls deep in the forest of his beard.

Or did he say, "Don't blow my cover"? But if so, it might be an act of trust, a way of saying, "I have some *miztvot* to perform, some mezuzahs on the cheap for those a little strapped, not in *tefillin*, but in the pocketbook, so be a good boy, even if you're old enough to be a grandfather, and button your lip."

As Ludwig pondered possibilities and innuendos, ambiguities and ambivalences – his academic field, if he had one – the learned man or *gonif*, maybe both, virtually climbed over Ludwig, nearly stepping on his balls.

"You should forgive me," he said, "I have people to meet."

"I'll bet you do," Ludwig said sotto voce, thinking, *maybe Russian Mafia, maybe West Bank connections.*

Still, it was good to be rid of the puritanical snorer who thought reading Philip Roth was worse than eating lobster and who was guilty probably of nothing worse than smuggling a few scrolls into Israel for resale in the Carmel Market. But maybe it was worse. Maybe he was carrying messages for some friends of Hamas.

Well, good riddance, he probably wouldn't see him again, and he could bid farewell to his paranoid fantasies. He would consider himself lucky if the semi-rebbe and super-nudnik stepped out of his life without crushing his macadamia nuts and vanished.

No such luck. As fate would have it, he was standing in front of the mystery man as they waited to have their entry forms collected and passports stamped. But the old man wasn't waiting. He was leaning and pushing against Ludwig again. His whiskers tickled the back of Ludwig's neck, but he wasn't tickled pink.

"So what would be so bad if you let me wiggle through, I got people waiting. You look like you could wait all day. You can read some more of that *drek* while you wait."

With this, he eased by Ludwig, a supple movement like Clyde the Glide that made him even more suspicious. For a second he looked like OJ sweeping the UCLA line in the days when he raised football to the level of art. And, like OJ, he might have something to hide – probably no blood on his hands, but anything was possible when small leather *tefillin* cases might be thought of as places to hide explosives.

"Stop him," Ludwig said, "stop the *schnorrer*, he's hiding something in his beard, don't let him fool you!"

"What's with you, crazy?" said a black-frocked man standing in back of Ludwig. "He's a man of the cloth, can't you see?"

"Seeing isn't believing with this guy, I know, I tell you he's hiding something in that cloudlike forest of his."

"He's talking clouds," someone said, "we better get security. Who knows what he's up to?"

A crowd circled around Ludwig, a mixture of tourists and security people, even a few IDF solders and, then, without knowing how they got there, he and the alleged rabbi were sitting at opposite ends of a table in a private room off to the side of the passport booths. Guards stood in each corner, holding semi-automatic weapons.

A young lieutenant, red-haired, who looked more Irish than Israeli, faced them. His uniform was rumpled, but his paratrooper's insignia was brightly polished.

"Now, boys," he said with a Brooklyn accent, "what seems to be the problem?"

132

"Boys?" they murmured to themselves and looked at one another.

"You both look like reasonable gentlemen, you don't look like troublemakers, it must be irritation after a long flight without enough legroom."

"He's the troublemaker!" each said, pointing at the other.

"He sits next to me and reads *drek*."

"He's smuggling something in his beard! I saw him roll them like joints all night!"

"Me, a smuggler? I'm as pure as Mount Hebron on a winter night."

With that, he ran his mottled hands through his beard and held the ends of the strands in his fingers.

"See, Mr. Lieutenant, I'm clean."

"He's hiding them," Ludwig said, "I saw those scrolls."

"Oh, the scrolls, why didn't you say so?"

With that he emptied his pockets, frayed with tufts of cotton pushing through the holes and put a pile of folded note paper on the table.

"See, I told you," Ludwig said, "cuff him, Lieutenant."

"Tell me, sir, what are these notes? Who are they for?"

"A nice Jewish boy here in Israel asks such a question? Well, if you must know, they're a collection of *kvittel* that I plan as soon as possible, if you'll let me go, to put in the *Kotel*, messages from my friends in Brooklyn who, though no anti-Semite would believe it, are too poor to travel to Israel."

"Please, let me see one," the lieutenant said.

"This I shouldn't do, but I got places to go."

He unraveled one note and placed it on the table: "From Ocean Avenue with love."

He opened another, "Go Buffalo sabras!"

"The guy's a real Borscht-belt comedian," Ludwig said.

"Next thing you know he'll be singing *There's a small kotel with a wishing wall*."

"Funny or not, he doesn't seem to be a troublemaker, and we'll both probably hear from some Yeshiva in Crown Heights about this. But we can't be too careful, you're right about that, so let's call it a day. Welcome to Israel and may you both have a safe and pleasant visit, *Shalom!*"

At the word "pleasant," Ludwig and the sit-down comedian looked at each other, if not with scowls than something less than amusement. It was clear to each that they would be happy never to see one another again, though they each had to admit to themselves, even if they wouldn't admit it to each other, that they must have something in common.

Why else would the two of them be visiting a country where there was a risk, even if slight, that a bomb might go off or a rocket land with shattering impact anywhere, any time? As Ludwig had written to a friend during the 2006 summer war, "Hezbollah wasn't aiming at me as I floated in the Kinneret, but then their aim wasn't very good."

Not that the IDF was always that accurate, either, but at least they tried to hit specific targets. In any case, after the Holocaust, he could forgive almost anything that Israel did to defend itself. The threat to the existence of a people, many of whom had little in common except the word "Jew," never could be set aside in Ludwig's mind as a motive for what Israel did.

His views weren't popular with quite a few Jewish academics with whom he rubbed elbow patches, but few of them had been to Israel in recent years, if at all. All they remembered was a good summer on a kibbutz during college before the '67 war, a dream they wanted to preserve. For them, Israel had been a vacation idyll which, when betrayed, felt like a self-betrayal. And Ludwig couldn't deny that there had been betrayals and worse, but he would have been lying if he said that they had become for him the equivalent of the terrors of the Final Solution. Why not ask the Japanese to "get over" Hiroshima or Germans Dresden?

Well, he wouldn't have to justify himself to anyone for a while, and he was unlikely ever to see the high-powered nudnik again for whom needling assimilated American Jews like Ludwig was a profession.

No such luck, again.

Waiting at the curb near the taxi rank outside Ben-Gurion, who should be almost standing next to him but the Chief Rabbi of the Grand Concourse or Shabbes goy in black gabardine! But not breathing down his neck, thankfully.

A pregnant Arab-Israeli or Palestinian en route to the West Bank, wearing a hijab and abaya, and her young daughter, sparkly-eyed and bouncy, stood between them. Though dressed in black, she smiled joyfully as she looked at her daughter skipping in place.

"Be patient, sweet girl," she said in BBC English, "we'll be home soon, if they treat us nicely."

She sounded like a modern woman and Ludwig wondered if she was wearing a Dior dress or naughty lingerie, see-through teddy, under her somber outer covering. It was getting harder and harder to know who was who and what they stood for, if anything. Most people were floaters, after all, as he knew all too well, having tread water in many lakes and ponds in his life, including the Big Muddy of his mind. He longed to learn the Australian crawl, without drifting, or to stand naked on a float so everyone could see who he was – a *dingle in sich*, of Whitman, a distant cousin.

If he had acted unambivalently in the past, it has been only in moments of sexual hi-jinx when he had lost himself and lost his sense of aloneness. He had felt cast adrift from childhood and only the thought of hot sex with an all-embracing woman, with or without candlelight, violins, and poetry, had seemed to promise a port of safe call, a harbor that protected him from feelings of isolation. He sailed under the flag of abandonment. In lean times, two years before MasterCard had kept him afloat.

The little girl patted her mother's stomach and moved her hand in a small circle.

"Yes, dear mother," she said, as if she were speaking in a fairy tale or had attended a nursery school in Cambridge, either one. For a perverse moment, he wondered if the woman really was pregnant.

Could she be wired with an IED? It made no sense, of course – she had been through security too many times. But what did "security" mean in this part of the world, or most parts, for that matter.

But it was a sign of the times that such fugitive thoughts even could pop into his head, as the loony fantasies about the possibility of scrolls being hidden in the rabbi's beard suddenly had jumped into his head like tiddlywinks, a game he had loved to play with David, along with sugar-packet table-top soccer. There was no getting away from it: there was no way to know what was going on in someone else's head in this instance or anywhere else. Philosophers had raised the question, he believed, "Can we know other minds?" It seemed clear to him that not only can we not know other minds, but we rarely, if ever, know our own.

Sartre's *"L'enfer, c'est les autres"* now wore boots, and they were on the ground in Israel and other troubled lands where the quest for identity was more powerful than the fear of being blown to smithereens. It could take just a nanosecond for Being to become Nothingness. He thought of Rajeev Gandhi, Benazir Bhutto, JFK, Martin Luther King, Jr. – stepping out for a smoke on a balcony in Memphis and now gone. For anyone interested in changing history, killing seemed to be the way to go. No exit was the way out.

Still, the little girl, with the Tiffany-diamond bright eyes, wouldn't have been touching her mother so tenderly if it was a danger zone, but then she could have been trained. After all, children had been killed all over the world for righteous causes. He thought of Viet Nam, photos of children running, in flames, being burned alive.

A taxi pulled up in front of the woman and child. Ludwig was pleased that the driver wasn't going to favor the *schnorrer* from Coney Island, whoever he was or wherever he was from, who seemed to think he was some kind of royalty with his *droit de seigneur* attitude towards everything. After all, he wasn't the Messiah, if there was one. But, then, who was to say he wasn't? You couldn't be sure. Christ had tried, poor guy, and look what happened to him!

Prophetic types, types claiming to be prophets, were wandering the streets in all major cities, even some small towns. One village south of Buffalo, Lillydale, specialized in prophecy: palm reading, crystal balls, Tarot cards, séances with the "other side" – the whole nine yards, more than the Bills usually gained. And you could turn on TV in America 24/7 and see some pomaded, coiffured, waxen faced preacher – with outstretched arms that looked like divining rods – appealing to the lame and defeated to declare for Christ, to be reborn. And some did and some were. For all Ludwig knew, *he* himself might be the Messiah, not that he ever had had such a crazy thought.

And what was literary criticism, French style, if not an

attempt, quite successful in most major American universities, to undo clarity of meaning? If Ludwig's generation had tried to make sense of experience in the aftermath of World War II, after the Holocaust and Hiroshima, the succeeding generations of literary academics, looking for a new form of rebellion, had turned to non-sense.

It didn't make a lot of sense to Ludwig, but many of his colleagues were living proof, or somewhat living proof, that a long Age of Reason had been turned upside down even as faculty salaries went up. The less sense you made, the more affluent you became. He would write Paul Krugman about this and see what he thought. It occurred to Ludwig that there should be an Ignobel Prize.

Just as the lady, holding her child's hand, reached to open the door of the taxi with her free gloved hand, the rabbi took a step towards the door and tried to push Ludwig aside.

"Excuse," he said, "I got people waiting for me."

"You're not excused," Ludwig said, "and this lady and her child were here first. Remember? Women and children into the lifeboats first."

"We're on our land, Mr. Wise-Guy, this isn't the *Titanic,* so you should excuse," and, as he said this, he tried to step into the taxi, but Ludwig held onto the tail of his coat, and the mystery man, suspended in air, arms outstretched to balance himself, looked like an overdressed angel – a Chagallian jester.

"Let go, you piece of *tref,*" the man yelled.

"Are you sure?"

"Let go."

With that, Ludwig released his grip, and the man hit the curb and bounced like a Slinky. The sturdy rim of his fedora broke the fall, but then rolled towards the woman and child.

The mother looked at Ludwig with a mixture of embarrass-
ment and fear as if she were responsible and would be
blamed, maybe even arrested. Ludwig, pleased, confused,
worried as well that the police might come and hold up his
trip to the Lower Golan, reached down to help the fallen man
to his feet.

"The Romans and the Nazis weren't enough for you, you
had to lend a hand," the toppled man said in a tremulous
voice.

All the color had gone out of the man's face and Ludwig's
heart began to race, afraid that he might have seriously hurt
him. Worse – that he had humiliated and rendered him helpless. In an instant, what had seemed almost comic now wore
a tragic mask. He saw in his night companion's face the look
of a man whose existence was threatened, as that of the Jews
had been for millennia.

He was worried for the man and himself. The last thing
he wanted was another scene that would cause a delay and
an interrogation. So far no one had noticed anything unusual
taking place amidst the hustle and bustle of the taxi rank.

"Look," Ludwig said, "you owe me an apology, and I owe
you one, but I'm in a hurry, too, so let's shake."

"What, I should touch a hand like yours that touched the
pages of Pupick Roth or whatever his name is."

"You could have worse enemies, believe me, but let's call
it a day. We've both got people to meet. I'll help you with
your luggage. You take this cab, and I'll help the woman and
child."

"Your smutty hands shouldn't touch my things," the man
said.

Ludwig took his hand off the suitcase. The extreme nudnik, Olympic class, might be an orthodox screwball, but he
had to respect him, no matter what. The dark figure picked

up his bags and entered the taxi. Ludwig thanked his lucky Star of David that he never had to see this Torah nutcase again. He heard Martin Luther King's words echo in his ear, "Free at last."

He smiled politely and bowed slightly towards the Arabic woman – Arab-Israeli? Palestinian? Jordanian? Who knew? He then hailed a taxi for her and pressed a hundred NIS into her gloved hand.

"For a tip," he said, "my apologies."

"I can't," she said.

"Please, not for the money, a peace-offering."

"For that, yes, thank you."

He then asked the driver to help her with her luggage. He was pleased to see that it was Louis Vuitton. As the taxi pulled away, she smiled and waved.

He had hoped to see his daughter's Israeli family, especially David, in clear light. It was winter, but it still might be bright and sunny, Rembrandt mellow. Now he would arrive in the evening. If he was lucky, the moon would be out.

He couldn't expect to see the boy, now at the edge of manhood, as he had seen him a few summers ago during a Shavo'ot festival.

David then had chased young girls in white blouses, who wore garlands of poppies and roses, around bales of hay. When David caught up with one and plucked a flower from her wreath, she had shouted with joy. All this took place under a sun so vividly golden and piercingly hot that Van Gogh might have cut off the other ear.

He couldn't expect such unalloyed joy now. The boy was older and the shadow of history was about to cross his path. Ludwig wasn't sure what he would feel now, or *even if he could stay* to face what he felt, but he needed to see them together, one family, like a Henry Moore statue, silhouetted

140

against the surrounding hills: Mount Arbel to the east, Mount Hermon to the north, not Kilimanjaro exactly, but something like it for him. He needed to see his only daughter and her chosen life in the full context of her life in the moshav.

He had seen them together before, of course, but this time it would be different because the eldest son, the one he had helped raise as an infant, would go into the IDF in a few years, especially at a time when there were rumblings again about another Intifada and a Hezbollah build-up along the Litani River across the Lebanon border.

There might not be another conflict like the one in the summer of 2006, but if there were, it would be worse, especially if Iran got into it. And then David might be one of the combatants. He remembered the greasy faces and dirty hands of the young men who had come back from the Litani front in 2006, and David's could be among them in the future.

It was a painful thought, and he wasn't sure he ever could face it and accept it. In some ways, he had been the boy's grandfather and father, and any injury to the boy would be felt doubly, if ever profound loss could be calibrated. And the boy's mother, his daughter, would be shattered, even as she had chosen to live in such a dangerous part of the world.

He wasn't sure if she had thought it through, but no matter what her thoughts were, they would be blown up in the face of any harm to her children. Marion had the heart of a mother-lion, and the first-born had the warrior spirit of the Lion of Judah. That was part of the problem.

It was a relief to sit, half-asleep in the back of the taxi, without anyone to annoy him. The ride north to Tiberias and beyond to the Golan had become almost a relaxing and comforting trip for him – so different from the first time, 2002, when he had flown into Tel Aviv during the Second Intifada, on edge all the time. He had felt lost then, driving north, not at all sure where Tiberias was and whether or not it was a city or a caravansary.

The darker the night sky became during that first trip, as the lights of Tel Aviv and the coastal towns – Netanya, Hadera – became dim, he had wondered how he would get out of this country, which had become his daughter's home-land but was not his home, if a full-scale conflict erupted.

Now, he became a little excited, even charmed, as the lights of Tiberias came into view past the Poriya Junction. Maybe the word "junction" had something to do with it; it reminded Ludwig of African-based safari movies, *Bhowani Junction, The Snows of Kilimanjaro*. Of course, Hem had haunted Ludwig for years – Hem and Henny Youngman were his crossroad, "Hemmy," his aka when it suited him.

Tiberias, once an unknown city in a remote part of the world, had become familiar to him, and the necklace of lights on its terraced hills now lit up his inner light bulb. This small city, whose sacred origins as site of the Sanhedrin had given way to tourism, had stepped out of the shadow of history for him and become a site of memory and feeling, reflection and retrospection.

He had sat at its scruffy cafés and noisy outdoor shawarma restaurants on bustling Habanim Street countless times, waiting for his daughter to finish her shopping, and he had had a hundred opportunities to review his life in the midst of loud music and noisy vendors. It was his daughter's town now and, for better and worse, to some extent, *his*.

Israel and Tiberias had imposed deeper layers of inward-ness upon him – not that he needed it. His psyche had become a virtual archeological site as a result of all his visits, not exactly a national antiquity, no Capernaum or Bet She'an, but important to Ludwig, keeper of his own archive and curio cabinet.

His heart beat faster as the taxi came out of the hills over-looking Tiberias and took the turn toward the Ma'agan Junction and then headed north along the eastern side of the Kinneret on Route 92 past Kibbutz En Gev, one of the pio-neer era settlements, along with Ginosar and Deganya on the shore of the Kinneret.

He could see in the twilight against the hills on the west-ern side of the Kinneret strings of lights that rimmed Migdal and Ginosar, historic birthplace of Mary Magdalene and staging area for Yigal Allon's Palmach unit. To Ludwig, the lights looked like the rigging and masts of motionless ships, a stationary flotilla that reminded him somehow of his own life: prepared for action, but too often becalmed. It was com-forting to look at the steady lights across the Kinneret. It was good when nothing dramatic happened in Israel, but you couldn't count on it for too long.

This was one of those quiet times when it was almost pos-sible for Ludwig to believe that he was living in the time of Jesus and the Sanhedrin on the shores of the Kinneret, a time to treasure the ripples on the Kinneret, rolling from the west to the east in the early twilight, and the fluttering of birds in the marsh-reeds that edged the lake.

This was as safe a place in Israel as any. If some group were going to fire a rocket or artillery shell, they might take some care not to hit the churches and sites of Christ's minis-try that ringed the lake. Which wasn't to say that the IDF or Hezbollah made reverence for holy sites a priority. Still, Ludwig felt pretty safe as the taxi approached the Kursi turn-off where an early Byzantine church was nestled within a grove of eucalyptus and cypress trees. So much history came together, then separated people.

And he felt even safer as the taxi headed up into the hills

towards the villages of Bene Yehuda and Giv-At Yo-Av where his daughter lived. These towns were only ten kilometers from the point where the Syrian and Jordanian borders met. Nonstrategically located, they only would come under attack during a full-scale war, and Syria wasn't looking for one now. And there were no displaced populations in the valleys between Israel and Syria. Of course, there was Ahmadinejad to worry about, but if Iran fired a long range rocket, it would mean something like a full-scale war, and few people would be safe anywhere. Still, their threat couldn't be discounted.

Ludwig asked the taxi driver to turn off the radio with the usual pop music blaring as the first curve approached that would bring Ludwig closer to his daughter and her family. He wanted to preserve this moment in memory, unsure how often and what intervals he would be able to visit Israel again. He was getting older, money was tight, and his daughter and husband had chosen a way of rural life that made it almost impossible for them to afford a visit to America with all their children.

And there were all the other issues he had thought about on the flight over, including the shadow of David's upcoming service in the IDF. Ludwig had lived with dark premonitions and apprehensions from the moment his daughter had decided to make Aliyah during the Intifada of 2002.

He focused on the twisting line of an old donkey trail, smooth chalky white, until he lost sight of it in the darkness of the Samakh River Valley. Once he and David had splashed in the narrow stream that ran through the reed-enclosed waters. He could see the lights of Kibbutz Gesher at the crest of the ridge, another stationary ship in the sea of the Golan Hills.

He had absorbed the contours of this landscape over the past decade. He wanted to fix the topography firmly in his mind. He remembered telling David, somewhat jokingly, a few years ago that the deep gouges in the hills were "the imprint of God's fingers," the eternal hand impressing itself upon the land.

He needed to tell David everything that seemed important to him before it was too late. The boy was growing up fast, and the speed was accelerating. He was a slightly different young man each time Ludwig visited. The boy's identity was unfolding in mysterious ways. Could anyone tell who David would become?

As the taxi wound its way up the hill, each turn put the landscape into a different perspective. At one point, he could see only the twilight sapphire-white sky above the ridge; at another, the Kinneret came into view, but not always the same arc of shoreline. At one twist, he could see Tiberias to the southwest; at the next one, he could see the crest of the orthodox and artistic city of Zefat to the northwest where Hassid and Parisian wannabes coexisted.

These different perspectives were not unlike his shifting attitudes towards the life his daughter had chosen for herself. They reminded him of the Peak Tram in Hong Kong and how each point of the rapid ascent put the Lego-maze of the city in a different configuration. He wished he could go back to those three years when he taught in Hong Kong before David's birth. Life had been less complicated, if lonelier, then.

His heart raced as the taxi headed into the sixteenth and last turn.

He still could see in the fading light the olive groves and vineyards that led to Offir Lookout where he had spent many dreamy hours but, like the lake below, his past ruminations had been circular.

He was pleased now that his arrival had been delayed, however upsetting the encounters with the annoying religious man had been. Now he would be able to see them for the first time, doubtless outside the house waiting for him, in the twilight and not at midday. The children would be at home, and Gil would have finished his tractor work for the day.

His daughter Marion, a "stay at home mom," as she would be called in America, would be there any hour of the day, and that was one of Ludwig's problems, if he had a right to have a problem with the life his daughter had chosen. After all, his own life hadn't exactly been the fulfillment of *his* father's dream of what Ludwig might become. He hadn't failed his father like Biff and become a wanderer, but he had drifted and shifted his center of gravity. His middle name could have been and still might be "If."

His grandfather had been a peddler on the Lower East Side: "Old clothes, I sell old clothes." His father had toiled in the canyons of the Garment Center on 37th Street, making enough money before bankruptcy became his occupation, to send Ludwig to college to become, his father hoped, a dentist, if not a doctor. His father had been "in" so many bankruptcies that when people asked him what business his father was in, he could have said, "bankruptcy."

But he had no manual dexterity and had fallen in love with words, not teeth or the colon (except as a punctuation mark), so he had cobbled together a life as a writer and teacher, with his father's help in the early years of near academic, if not genteel, poverty with miniscule royalties. His writing earned him less than a set of dentures, but still he had been able to send Marion to college in the hope that she would be able to lead an independent and professional life.

Like most parents, he wanted her to be more successful and secure than he had been, as proof in part that he had raised her carefully and intelligently. The fear of poverty and the inability to escape some nightmare of history was never far from his New York version of the Jewish mind.

If bigots wanted to know, as a form of accusation, why Jews seemed to be successful, a simple answer might be that the threats of boots in the face, exile, and extinction ignited the fire of ambition. Maybe, over time, some had inherited a mutant Madoff gene. And sometimes it had been a real fire or worse: great uncle Fried's harness store in Bohemia had been ransacked in 1942, and then he had disappeared, only to be discovered in 1994 in a dossier with the date of his extermination at Terezin.

He wanted his daughter to be clear about the implications and possible consequences of her choices and to pay for them, to be able to protect herself and her children in case he wasn't able to help her. His resources were limited, and then one day he would be gone. Once he had asked her how she would feel when he went to work out for the last time in the big Jewish Center in the sky, and she had said, "Helpless."

It pained him to think that he wouldn't always be able to help her financially. Immodest ambitions and a low income were a terrible combination if you wanted to provide for your children into an uncertain future. And he, mini-big shot, had decided as a high school student that he would take the high mountain road to literature rather than the low road to dental school. Better to set sail for the Panama Canal than drill into a root canal.

He hadn't factored in what it might mean some day to bring a child, who might have children, into a dangerous world. His father never had used the world "family," so it hadn't been part of Ludwig's vocabulary.

Coming of age in the affluent postwar period, he had assumed that the world would be his oyster and that he'd be able to slurp it down even if it wasn't kosher. America was expanding in all directions, seemingly without limit, and he assumed that he would be part of it and could have it all. He could have his shellfish *tref* and eat it, too.

He had walked across the George Washington Bridge one summer evening after his high school graduation with the exhilarating sense that his prospects were as wide and open as the span of the great bridge and the receding vistas of the Hudson River, north to West Point, south to Lady Liberty.

No lover of heights, he had risen above his anxieties for a few moments, suspended in the illusion that he could act on his literary ambitions and lead something like the secure and somewhat glamorous life that many of his affluent Park Avenue and Central Park West classmates would be able to live. He could keep these thoughts at bay when he was home, but they came to the fore every time he landed at Ben-Gurion Airport and walked down the long ramp, dragging a suitcase full of gifts, back aching, knowing that he could be in Israel for weeks, or months, if a major conflict erupted.

Arriving finally at Giv-At Yo-Av, he asked the taxi driver to stop at the bottom of the hill leading to his daughter's house. He paid the bill, stepped out, and sat on his suitcase in the shadow of a stand of cypress trees.

The sturdy upright branches didn't flutter in the cool breeze. Cool for Ludwig, of western New York winters, a denizen; but for Israelis, cold, children of scorching summers and parched earth. For him, a relief from winter's ravages; for them, without central heating, the need to gather wood for the stove.

He and Marion, her family, were clearly of two worlds now, bound together, but separate. He breathed deeply. He didn't want to communicate any discomfort, confusion, or anxiety when he saw them. He had come too far without frequent flyer miles to tip them off about the turbulence of his inner life. He had landed safely. It made no sense to tell them about his bumpy inner journey.

There was a row of cypress trees on a steep grade leading up to their house. The cedar porch of their house, the one Gil had built, looked down over the peak of these evergreens, and no one would be able to see him until he popped out like Woody Allen in *Zelig* from behind the last one. And even then they wouldn't be able to see him, if he crouched, until he actually stepped onto their porch. The wire fence around the house was covered with the climbing morning glory he had bought and planted for them.

He was breathing quickly now and had to approach slowly to calm himself down. It was absurd to be hiding from them, having come so far, like a juggler who didn't want to toss a third ball in the air. But, then, that was what it meant, in part, to be Ludwig Fried.

As he approached the last tree in the row, he could see the glow of their grill through the foliage of the fence. It was Shabbat, and Gil liked to treat the family to schnitzel, his favorite dish, on this special evening. It pleased him that Gil, who worked so hard that he collapsed after work wherever he was sitting or lying, took the time to show his family what his labors were for: to satisfy their needs, to make them feel safe, to give the word "family" a special meaning for them.

At the same time Ludwig was pleased that he was still far enough away so that he heard only the murmur of their voices: Marion, Gil, David, Ben, and Jacob. Like most Israelis, Marion's family was noisy. It was hard to find a quiet spot, especially on the crowded beaches and beach clubs around the Kinneret where Israeli and Arab-Israeli pop music filled the air.

There had been many times at dinner at Marion's, with children screaming and virtually throwing falafel balls at one another, when he had thought of leaving. But he had restrained himself. It was *her* family. He hadn't come this far to interfere in her life. He had to remember: *this was her chosen life*, even if he didn't feel that he was one of the chosen people. He listened carefully. It was strangely quiet. He pressed his ear against the leaves of the morning glory vine and branches of a fig tree. One of the figs rested, like a dreidel, on the tip of his nose.

"Now, boys, listen to your older brother." It was Marion's voice. "David wants to talk to you and, David, speak to them in English, they have to learn English, too."

"Okay, Mom. Now, boys, Grandpa will be coming soon, and when he comes, I want you to be real quiet. No screaming. He's come a long way, and he'll want to talk to us. So, we've got to listen, at least until tomorrow."

There was laughter and giggles. David, now sixteen, sounded more mature than he had just a year ago. At his stage of life, a year could mark more of a change than a decade would at a later time in his life.

"Ben, Jacob, do you understand?"

"Will he bwing presents?" they shouted in unison.

"First of all, don't shout, second, Grandpa *is* the present."

"We want presents," they repeated, somewhat lower in volume, but still loud.

"Ok, boys," Marion said, "I've got a great idea, let's take a photo of the whole family on the tractor before Grandpa comes. We can print it out on the computer and give it to him as a present when he arrives. What do you think, Gil?"

"It's a good idea," her husband said, "Ludwig will like it,

150

he likes art," he said with a mixture of irony and admiration.

The five of them disappeared for a minute. Then pressing his nose against the fence, Ludwig could see all of the boys and Gil sitting on the giant tractor with floodlights at the sides of the green and yellow John Deere machine. They cast their silhouettes against the tall wall of the house, the house Gil, not Babe Ruth, had built from the ground up. Marion stood below them, pointing her camera up at them.

It was the first time he had seen the John Deere machine that had changed their lives and reduced his retirement income. Gil had sent him the brochure for the scraper tractor with a scrawled note, the only one he ever had written in English to Ludwig: "We need your help. Please help. Our life will be different."

He couldn't forget the note. It had been so touchingly simple and had cost Ludwig so much. He dreaded to think what "attachments" Gil would need in the years to come, if he could make a living on the Golan and if the Golan even would remain part of Israel. Ludwig needed attachments, too, but of a different kind. Each man needed his own kind of attachment: *chaucun son attachement.*

They could have stepped out of a 1940 Israeli poster he once had seen for a "Redeem the Land" stamp with the seven Biblical species in the foreground against what looked like the hills of the Golan: wheat, barley, vines, fig, pomegranate, grape, and olive, *"ein Land darin es Olbaume und Honig gibt."* Gretchen, his old flame, who had singed him finally, had taught him the German for milk and honey as a symbolic act of reparation. It had been a touching parting gesture.

"A little closer," Marion said.

As Gil, sitting between the great wheels, put his sun-burnt arms around David, and David put his slightly muscular teenage arms around Ben and Jacob, the snapshot turned into something like a Soviet poster of the years before the show-trials when it still was possible for intellectuals and writers in the West to think that the USSR was building a new land for a new people just as Herzl thought possible for Jews in Turkish Palestine. A time before Isaac Babel was imprisoned and later murdered. Stalin's sadistic lackeys even had broken the writer's eyeglasses.

"Okay, boys, say '*sabra*'!"

"What's 'sabwa,' Mommy?"

"What the two of you are," Marion said, "children who were born here."

"But you borned us," Ben said.

"Me, too," Jacob echoed.

It made no sense to wait any longer. He tip-toed onto the porch and made a shush gesture to Gil and the boys as he approached Marion who was concentrated in getting the group in focus, but the two small boys began to yell and to jump up and down.

"Gwanpa, Gwanpa...."

"He's coming," Marion said, "be still."

"He's here," Ludwig said as he stepped in front of Marion and hugged her.

"You're here, Dad, you're finally here."

"Did you think I was coming to see Damascus?"

The boys began to climb off the tires.

"Stay there, boys, let's get Grandpa into the picture."

"Can these old bones make it?"

"You'll never be stooped," David cried out, "come on up."

"Yes, Ludwig, it's time you became a farmer," Gil chimed in, "you can show your friends what Israel looks like when we're not at war."

Ludwig clambered onto the tractor. He had received a few

"Dear Johns" in his life, but he never had been on a John Deere.

"You sit in the middle, Grandpa," David said.

Ludwig knelt between Ben and Jacob, arms around them. David crouched behind Ludwig and put his arms on Ludwig's shoulders. Gil, who could have played power forward for Maccabi Tel Aviv in the early days before American and European players began to crowd out the Israelis, reached around David and spread out his arms to embrace them all.

"Hold still, now," Marion said, "say 'chutzpah.'"

She held the camera steady and clicked.

"What about you, Mom?" David said.

"Another evening, boys, when Grandpa's rested. He's come a long way."

They stepped off the tractor and stood in a circle as if they were about to do the hora, especially poignant because the hora was now a dance of the past, the time of the pioneers, not the Intifada.

"Well, how do they look?" Marion asked quietly.

"It's a joy to look at them."

"That's such a nice thing to say, Dad, it makes it worth it to stay here."

"It's the truth, Marion."

"Well, we've got to get you settled in your house on the kibbutz."

"Is it the one hanging over the gorge?

"Yes, all the old ones are near the edge at Gesher. It made it easier to defend in 1948, but we got a good price for you. Gil will drive you over after you've given the children their presents and they've gone to bed.

She winked at him, "We'll get the rental car in Tiberias in the morning."

"The presents, of course. That's all I've brought except

socks and underwear."

"Don't worry, we have all your stuff put neatly away."

"We want presents…we want presents."

"Mommy will give them to you," he said, handing the valise to Marion.

"I'll drive you over later," Gil said, "I've got to fix the gate at a moshav down the road."

Ludwig was pleased he had arrived after Shabbat. Marion and Gil didn't make a fuss about it, but he knew that David was becoming more involved in the ceremony, and he didn't want to embarrass him by not being able to say the prayers properly in Hebrew, his bar mitzvah trauma redux.

He still recalled with some anxiety how nervous he had been when he stood on the Bimah of Ansche Chesed on West End Avenue and faced his relatives and father's Garment District cronies, all of whom knew more about Judaism than he ever could know. They were children of Europe, greenhorns. He was just a greenhorn: summer camp, Central Park West parties, college quadrangles.

With Marion opening the presents and Gil off on his tractor for an hour or so, he would have a chance to talk a little with David and try to find out what his grandson was thinking. With the younger boys busy at putting together a Lego set and Marion watching them so that they didn't try to put a piece in the other boy's ear, Ludwig followed David into his room where he wanted his grandfather to listen to some Beatles songs.

"I've just discovered them, Grandpa, they're the best. Their songs make sense. I don't like hard rock or heavy metal."

"I always liked 'Here Comes the Sun'," Ludwig said, "I think Shakespeare and Bialik would have liked it, too."

"Where were you in the 1960's, Grandpa?"

"I was too old to be drafted into the army for Viet Nam, so I enlisted in graduate school. It was a lot safer. But that was a long time ago, David, tell me about yourself, I haven't seen you in a year."

"Well, I break off with a girl every six months."

"I know the feeling, David. You're never too old to break up. I don't recommend it, but it happens."

"And I think I'm getting more serious, Grandpa.

"Don't rush it, you have a long life ahead of you."

"Really, Grandpa, be serious."

"Okay, tell me."

"Well, I've been reading Maimonides."

"I've only looked at the *Guide for the Perplexed.*"

David laughed, "I know that can help you, Grandpa, but I've been reading his *Book of the Commandments*, and I'm interested in what he has to say about 'duty' and the 'law.' I'm trying to figure out which of the 613 mitzvahs are the most important ones."

"What about Spinoza?"

"He's too complicated. I just like Maimonides. You know what they used to say in Tiberias at the time he was buried here."

"What?"

"From Moshe of the Torah to Moshe Maimonides there was none like Moshe."

"Sounds like one of my father's old partners."

"Be serious, Grandpa. Rambam is important."

"So is Baba Rum."

"Grandpa!"

"So what have you learned so far?"

"Well, I think he needed to add mitzvah number 614."

"Which is?"

"Your grandfather means well, but don't listen to everything he says, no one has all the answers."

They laughed and high-fived.

"Here, Grandpa," he put a headset on Ludwig, "listen, it's Paul."

"Saint?"

"Grandpa!"

He listened and was carried back to those days when all the people he knew were trying to reinvent themselves, including himself. People weren't interested in the past or present, only the future. They talked about the "now" and said "wow" if they thought they were in it, but they all knew that their new Now could only last in an imagined future if the Nixons of the world and the Joint Chiefs of Staff had conversion experiences.

"Guess what, Grandpa?"

"Tell me."

"I think I have better values now that I've been reading Maimonides."

"I can believe it, David, though I don't think you needed to improve a lot, especially compared to kids your age in America. They're too busy watching 'American Idol' and tweeting to one another to develop any values."

"C'mon, Grandpa, we have cell phones and iPods, too."

"Of course, but you're reading Maimonides."

"Well, some of the time."

"In fact, it's getting late, so I'll let you read some more while I wait for Gil to come back. I'll sit on the porch."

"Won't it be a little chilly?"

"Not for me, besides, spring is coming, it started a few days ago."

"What will we do tomorrow, Grandpa?"

"We'll go into Tiberias, pick up the car at Eldan, and then

do some shopping, whatever you need."

"They have some good buys at the *souk*, Grandpa."

"Then we'll go to the *souk* – *souk* and ye shall find."

"Grandpa!"

"Sorry."

He touched David lightly on the forehead, a blessing, such as he could muster for the spot where David might be placing *tefillin* (Ludwig wasn't sure), blew a kiss to Marion on the way out, and sat on the porch, waiting for the tractor to roll into the gravel driveway. It was a pleasant, winter evening. The rains hadn't come yet, and he had seen only a trace of snow on Mount Hermon to the north on the drive up.

Hermon wasn't Kilimanjaro, and Ludwig was no Hemingway, but it felt somewhat adventurous to be so close to *the* important mountain in this part of the world. Troops from three countries were garrisoned at its base – Lebanon, Syria, and Israel. It was the only good place for skiing in Israel, but a tough post for the IDF soldiers who stood guard at night near the summit, especially in winter when the army needed heavy equipment to keep the trails and roads open.

It was still light enough to see some of the fields in the valley below Marion's village. He could imagine how pleasurable it must feel for the Israeli workers who had tilled the fields in the scorching summer heat to know that the rains soon would come to justify their labors. Many Thai and Philippine workers now did the tending of the kibbutz and moshav fields, but there still were children of the pioneers and new immigrants – even some righteous Germans and Finns – who believed that working the land was the best way to live.

And he could imagine the jealousy and rage that some Syrian elders must feel when they recalled the days when their land overlooked the Kinneret, *their* "Buhairet

Tabariyya," who could see in their dreams the olive and lemon groves, the shade of the ficus trees, and the minaret thrust of the cypress. He could imagine the longing they must feel to return to this land of their origins as Jews in the Diaspora had dreamed of a return to a homeland, but he believed that history had given Israel no other hand to play.

He didn't expect any Syrian to agree with him. He understood that, too. He understood the other side, but they were the other side, the side David would have to face. And this is what had bothered him for a long time. He always would be on David's side, no matter what. Family was one thing, politics another. He could try to be fair, just, a universal man, the best Ludwig Fried possible, but his heart belonged to the survival of Marion and her family. It was a prejudice that he couldn't overcome, something deeper than a sense of justice. That was part of the problem – there was something deeper than values.

The lake was shaped like a "kinnor," Hebrew for harp, he had learned, even as he had learned little Hebrew since his bar mitzvah. In whatever language that was their own, the name of the lake was music for all those who had lived on its banks and the surrounding hills from the days of Herod Antipas, son of Herod the Great, in 17 BCE to the troubled present. The lake was the calm center of a troubled water over which no political bridge could be built.

Nothing could be settled, including settlements, until both sides, and there were more than two, recognized that they lived in an unsettled world. Borders couldn't be fixed so long as all sides believed in eternally fixed borders.

Maybe there was a simpler solution. If different sides stopped wearing head coverings and hats, or exchanged them periodically, no one could be sure who was who, and so the mayhem might stop. Or if they wore hats of neutral

nations such as Sweden and Switzerland, maiming and killing might seem especially arbitrary and thus obscene. Why
not bring back the fez and start history in this part of the
world all over again? It also would give the Turks a chance
to relive some empiric grandeur, and the Arabs and the Israelis a chance to reconsider an idealistic one-state solution,
however doomed such a project would be.

If the yarmulke could be exchanged for the *yagmurluk*,
the Jordan River might begin to flow south to north, so mi-
raculous would it be. If that was too threatening to both
sides, the *kippah* might be exchanged for a Gatsby and the
beanie for a montera. The possibilities were myriad: a kova
tembel, that shleppy Chico Marx cap, for a ghutrah, a pakul
for a kolpik – it seemed to be such a simple solution, *seemed*.
But he was drifting again, free association against the current, and he wasn't even wearing a Gatsby.

He saw a glimmer of light in David's window, and he
wanted to take a peek at his grandson before Gil returned.
He wanted to fix an image in his mind that always would be
there: a sixteen year old, still with a touch of boyhood, but
all the potentialities of manhood inscribed on his face.

He still had the faint smile, a touch of whimsy, that he had
at birth; thick brown eyebrows that contrasted with his aqua-
marine eyes, as if the land and the sea were mixed in him, a
forecast of the life that he would lead one day in the hills of
the Lower Galilee. And his body conveyed the doubleness
of his life as well: feet too large for his still growing body,
fat turning into muscle each day as he helped Gil load the
tractor with bags of cement.

No less than his grandfather Ludwig, David lived now, at

least for a while, in at least two worlds at once. The trick, it occurred to Ludwig, was to be able to lead those mixed and sometimes mixed up lives without breaking. Fitzgerald had it right in *The Crack-Up*.

But Ludwig wasn't sure if that was possible for him anymore. He wasn't getting any younger. He wasn't sure how long he could try to live in two worlds at once. He could still roam and float, but one of these days, he would simply plotz. And where did he want to be when he preferred the comfort of a lounge chair to the departure lounge at JFK?

Marion was putting increasing pressure on him, "C'mon, Pop, the time has come for you to be with your family, to move to Israel. It's where you belong, with us."

"I need some time, Marion, there are many things I need to think about."

It would be impossible to make her understand the equal weights on each side of his psychological scale. She would need someone from the Bureau of Standards to help with his teeter-totter sensibility: Henry James with sauerkraut on one side and hummus on the other. It was simple for her: he was her father and it was her duty to take care of him when he became infirm. But if she had lived inside his head for the past twenty-four hours, she would understand more than she would want to know and probably would want to change location.

"Well," he had said, "if I do come to live here when I can't putter in my own garden anymore, the boys can carry me around the Kinneret in a sedan chair. I can be the first Jewish rajah to make an appearance on the Galilee. If I can't walk on the water, I at least can be carried around it."

"Another of your great ideas, Pop, but at least you'd be here."

Like most daughters of a certain age, she made some

sense when it came to her father's well-being as he approached the end of days. Once she had been too young to be left alone, but soon he might be too old to be on his own. And where did he want to be? To be in upstate New York or to be in Israel? That was a question Hamlet might have asked of the AAA.

He tip-toed to David's window and peeked over the sill. He could see the flickering of a video game on David's computer. The boy had been playing them since he was five years old. Ludwig was pleased in a way that David was still connected to his childhood, but he was worried as well. He wanted David to become serious about his studies. Israel was a competitive society, and if David was going to go to university after the army, he had to start preparing himself now.

And then he noticed, in the soft glow of a lamp to the side of the computer, that David had a large book opened in front of him. His head bowed, wearing a blue velvet *kippah*, he was moving his fingers along the lines and mouthing words. Ludwig could read the author's name on the binding: *Maimonides*.

Ludwig couldn't decide if he looked more like a figure in a Rembrandt or a Vermeer painting. The subject was closer to Rembrandt, but the color values were more like Vermeer. In this moment, David looked more like a scholar than Ludwig ever had been in his years as a graduate student when all he had wanted to do was to get through with a degree and land a job.

He didn't want David to see him, and as he turned away, he saw the lights of Gil's tractor at the end of the road. It pulled closer.

"Grab your suitcase and climb up," Gil said, "I'll take you over to the kibbutz so you can get settled."

"Should I say good night to Marion?"

"She probably fell asleep with the children. She likes to do that. C'mon."

Ludwig clambered up, put his suitcase behind the driver's seat, and wedged close to Gil on top of an empty ammunition box.

"Don't work the shovel," Gil said, "it might break up part of the road."

"Don't worry, I don't have a clue, I only can operate a standard shift."

They rumbled smoothly out of the driveway, past the gate of the moshav, and soon were on the main road to Gesher. Though close to the town of Bene Yehuda, the kibbutz was isolated, bordered on one side by a gorge that opened into the Kinneret and on the other by orange, lemon, and olive groves.

As soon as the tractor rolled past the roundabout that connected the village of Bene Yehuda and the turn to moshav Giv-at Yo-av, they could see only the high beams on the road and clusters of lights where kibbutzim and religious communities were scattered in the Lower Golan. They looked like illuminated ports on a sparsely populated coast.

Everything else around them was shrouded in darkness, but he was confident that Gil knew where he was going and how to get there without driving into a ditch. Gil's hands were firm on the wheel.

"It's a good life here, Ludwig."

"You're at the top of the world, that's for sure."

"If it wasn't for the West Bank, Hezbollah, Syria, and Iran, it would be perfect," he said with a smile.

"At least you don't have to worry about the rest of the Moslem world."

"Not for now," Gil said, "but who knows?"

"So what about the future, Gil, the children, Marion?"

"This is our home, we'll do whatever we can to keep it unless the government tells us to leave. If that happened, I probably wouldn't want to live in Israel anymore. It would be the end of my grandfather's dream, the one who planted Rothschild's vineyards in Zichron Yaakov."

"Is there enough of the dream left, Gil? You know what all the boys will have to face, and David only has two more years before he goes into the IDF."

"No matter what, Ludwig, as dangerous as it can be, this is the only safe place for a Jew to be. At least we can defend ourselves."

"Safer than New York City?"

"Remember 9/11? Besides, I can't use my tractor there."

They passed through the gates of Gesher and stopped in front of one of the stucco cottages.

"The kibbutz manager, Moishe, lives here with his wife and two sons. Just knock, he's expecting you and will take you to your cottage. I'll pick you up in the morning with David. He wants you to take him shopping in Tiberias before you pick up the car at Eldan. He needs lots of things."

"Are you sure the manager is expecting me?"

"Sure."

"Ok, see you in the morning."

Ludwig climbed down. Gil slightly lifted and lowered his shovel as if to wave goodbye and rolled away.

He was a little embarrassed to have a suitcase instead of a knapsack or a duffle bag. It made him feel like a weekend guest at a hotel in the Borscht Belt, the few notches of it that were left, Scaroon Manor now a state park, or worse: a fake post-World War II refugee who had managed to make it through the British blockade to Haifa.

Nothing was worse, if you were an American-born Jew, than to pretend that anything you called "suffering" had anything to do with the fate of Jews during the Nazi period. Against this background, his suffering was only comic, and he suffered only in comparison.

For him, to make a short-list: suffering had been preparing for his bar mitzvah, never scoring a touchdown on his high school football team, dating mixed-up daughters of psychotherapists, trying to pay a spate of therapists (one hadn't been enough), trying to get published, being dumped by a beautiful younger woman who had ditched him for a more successful writer – "if you become successful, I may regret what I'm doing," – the words were chiseled on the façade of his soul.

Suffering had been these things for him and spending some sleepless nights decades ago wondering if publications in *The Saranac Review*, *Unconscious Quarterly*, and *Glitch* would get him tenure. They had. Then he had suffered a little when he knew he probably would spend the next twenty or thirty years at the same university shoveling snow in the winter and chipping icicles as thick as organ pipes off the eaves of his house. No E. Power Biggs, he was Ludwig Fried Digs. The modesty of his house, compared to those offered in the real estate section of *The New York Times*, also had caused him some grief: envy, jealousy, the sense that he had failed to get the middle class message – acquire, possess, assets, provide – even as he prided himself on being something of an outsider in an America where FOX News could make him feel like an alien.

But all these things, added together, didn't make up a Big Ticket item of grief and would have been embarrassing to think about, not to say mention, at Yad Vashem. Until Marion made Aliyah, Ludwig had thought he was about as Jewish as a Quaker was Christian or a Bahai'i Moslem, if either sect had a sense of humor. Now he was less certain about all of this, though he knew he wasn't a candidate for a Jerusalem Prize. Still, he was entitled to his history.

As a French friend of his, Roget de Gourmet, a gastronomical existentialist once had said, *"Je suis mon croissant."* Most of Roget's history had been spent sitting at a café near the Sorbonne, but it had been *his* history. He had coffee stains on his black turtleneck to prove it. You had to accept your history and make the most of it. Identity was a thesaurus – you picked your synonym, or it was chosen for you.

Ludwig understood all of this in a flash, like the explosion of an IED, when he had learned about the "death" in 1942 of the original Ludwig Fried, his great-uncle, at Terezin. "Death" was as good a word as any. None were adequate. After such knowledge, he no longer could see any aspect of his own life in a tragic light, no matter how hard he had tried, and he had tried in many cities in his twenties and thirties to convince a number of therapists that he deserved a place in the Freudian Hall of Fame located next to Temple Emanu-El on Fifth Avenue. It took the combined vote of fifty rabbis, therapists, and Dr. Phil "to go in." He didn't think he would make the cut.

And he had tried to seduce many women by telling them that only they could make him feel safe, "embosomed for a season in nature," as Emerson says in his Introduction to *Nature* (no true scholar, Ludwig still felt obliged to acknowledge writers when they came into his mind and gave them the right words, especially the great Emerson). But that had made him only a *schnorrer*, not a victim.

This had been one of the important discoveries of his late manhood: no matter how much angst he might claim, he remained a semi-comic figure. This certainly had been true of his life in America, but it was rapidly becoming less the case in Israel. And that was his immediate problem. His own military duty years ago as a "six-monther" had been a joke – trained as a surveyor and then assigned to hand out light-bulbs in an antiquated armory in Upper Manhattan every Monday night as a member of an Army Reserve unit. After all, how often did bulbs burn out, and what did you do while you waited? If you were Kafka or Beckett, it might be philosophically droll, but there was no comic side to David's upcoming military service in the IDF.

He waited outside the manager's cottage where only a porchlight beamed into the surrounding darkness. The Gamla gorge was a black sea to the northeast, and the Kinneret only could be inferred by the sparse lights of the kibbutzim that seemed to pulse like glow-worms across the lake. It lifted his spirits somewhat to see a tiara of lights on the crown of the ridge at Zefat, one of the four sacred cities of Israel, twenty miles to the northwest, glowed in the night-sky like a UFO.

These glimmers, in the midst of the darkness, were a match for the double state of his mind: inner and outer, waves of thought colliding with the whitecaps on the Kinneret, a montage of past and present, Jewish life in the Diaspora contra Jewish life in *Eretz,* his daughter as a child, now a mother, David an infant, now about to bear, unbearably, arms.

Ludwig didn't have to be Descartes or Freud to know that the mind was one thing and experience another and that it wasn't always easy to disentangle these realms of Being, if "being" was the right word. When it came to the essence of existence, to turn Sartre on his head, labels didn't work. Labels were good for coats and suits, this he had learned from his father, but the mind wasn't Fried and Barse, 7th Avenue, even if you shopped there. Treading water, drifting, again.

He knocked at the door, met the manager, and was shown to his cottage.

Later the next morning, he and David stood shoulder to shoulder at the side of the crowded entrance to the outdoor *souk* in Tiberias, a somewhat broken down collection of temporary sheds and stalls with tarpaulin canopies to protect against the sun and rain. The market always was busy, so there was no incentive for the merchants to put any money into refurbishing this bazaar. Besides, it had some charm for tourists, and then there were the intermittent intifadas which, though there hadn't been any violent conflicts in Tiberias, more or less closed the shops until the threat of violence across the country subsided. Now was a peaceful period, an interval between violence.

Although Ludwig and David no longer held hands – the boy was sixteen and aware of his emerging manhood, self-conscious and proud – David still felt comfortable standing close to his grandfather. Sometimes he even leaned against Ludwig during a scary moment when they went to the movies together. It was a natural outgrowth of their bond, one that had started when the boy was only eight months old. The boy couldn't remember a time when he didn't feel close to his grandfather, and Ludwig didn't want to think that a time would come when David would become embarrassed by the closeness between them.

In the interval between boyhood and manhood, mysterious and complex forces were at work, and no one really understood how an adolescent got from one place to another, but Ludwig knew that he had to respect the changes in David's life, to say nothing of his own.

"So tell me what you think you want before we try to push through the crowd, so we'll know which stalls to look at."

"Jeans and a scent, I think."

"A 'scent'?"

"You know, Grandpa, what you call cologne, I think."

"What kind?"

"Yours, *Old Spice.*"

"You remember?"

"Of course."

Although winter, it was a warm morning and there were no rain clouds in sight, a mixed blessing since good spring crops in the Golan depended on two months of rain, so the market was crowded with Israelis and Arab-Israelis, including some Druze villagers and even the odd Samaritan and Bedouin who came down to Tiberias from the Hermon area on market days.

"Let's count all the languages before we go in, Grandpa."

"Okay."

"Let's take turns."

"Hebrew."

"Russian."

"Arabic."

"Ethiopian, Grandpa."

"Thai."

"How do you know that one?"

"I was there once."

"Spanish, Grandpa, there are lots of Argentineans here."

"It's a big small world here, David, larger than I thought when I first visited."

"It's our world, Grandpa, and that's what's important."

"*Our* is a big word, David, but we can talk about it later. We've got to get your shopping done so we can pick up the car. They're expecting me at Eldan."

Having named the languages, the *souk* became more interesting to Ludwig, *a little United Nations,* he thought, and then he had to smile when he saw three UN soldiers with

French tricolor badges in the middle of the crowd near a falafel stand.

"Looks safe, cross your fingers," Ludwig said, "okay, let's go in."

Then, out of the corner of his eye, he saw, to his surprise and dismay, the rogue rabbi who had vexed him so much on the night-flight and then at Ben-Gurion.

"No, it can't be him," he said, as he pulled David aside.

"Who, Grandpa, what's the matter?"

"It's him, the fake rabbi."

"But he can't be fake if he's a rabbi."

"Believe me, he's fake, at least I hope he's a fake."

"Grandpa!"

"Just wait, let him go into the crowd. I won't make a scene."

"Well, that's good."

They stood shoulder to shoulder under the canopy of an Arab-Israeli fabric store as the broad rim of the rabbi's hat moved deeper into the crowd. He soon could see only the hat, as if it had a life of its own, an Israeli version of *Curious George*. Then a small group of Arab-Israeli teenagers who stood around him, almost as if they intended to encircle him, stepped aside, and Ludwig could see him standing alone.

It seemed odd to see anyone so distinctly standing alone in an Israeli open market. Ludwig had wiggled through them in Tel Aviv, Akko, Nazareth, and Jerusalem, and he never had felt any open space around him. It puzzled him. He thought of the incident at the beach two summers ago when a group of Israeli teenagers had taunted an Arab-Israeli at prayer.

He even had written a story about it, one of a series he had been working on for six years about the inescapable comedy of American Jewish experience against the background of the European tragedy, if tragedy was the right word. No word was the right word, no word was the final word, but as Elie Wiesel always pointed out, you had to keep trying to express the inexpressible.

With luck, this series would be his breakthrough book after all these years, the one that would bag a "book deal," NY style, with enough of an advance to buy Gil the excavator he needed, along with the tractor, to become a minor builder on the Golan, not unlike a certain version of Ludwig's own life. The narrow blade of the excavator could dig trenches for pipes and foundations where the tractor's claw was too wide to scope. With only the tractors, Gil was like a dentist with only one bit for his drill or a writer with a limited vocabulary – well, Hem was an exception.

Suddenly, the teenagers began to run, and there was a loud pop, a burst of flame, and a plume of smoke.

"Duck, Grandpa," David screamed, pulling his grandfather to the ground.

Ludwig felt his head with a free hand to see if it still was there.

"Help, help," a man cried. It was unmistakably the voice of his shady night flight companion.

"Oh, my god, maybe they've killed him, we've got to help," Ludwig said.

"Wait, Grandpa, there could be another explosion."

"No, we've got to help."

"Grandpa, let's get out of here."

"We can't run away."

Ludwig pulled himself free of David's grip and slowly approached the fallen man. If there was another explosive device, it probably would have gone off already. The man was writhing, moving his arms and legs in all directions, more hysterical, it seemed, than severely wounded, but there was a small pool of blood around his right hand.

Ludwig cupped his hand around the man's head to make sure there was no bleeding there, and then, gently picking up the man's hand, saw to his horror that his index finger had been blown or burnt off in the small blast, probably a large firecracker or small Roman candle. He took the bandana he always carried and wrapped it around the man's hand.

"David, quick, use your cell phone call the police and Magen David Adom!"

He could see that a number of people were calling already. In what seemed less than a minute, he heard several sirens and saw several flashing lights at the entrance to the *souk*.

The man now opened his eyes, as if he had been afraid to see what might be left of him.

"It's okay," Ludwig said, "you'll be okay, it's not a serious injury, here, let me help you sit up."

"It's you, the *gonif,* a person like you shouldn't touch me."

"Look, we're in the same boat here."

"First it was a plane, now it's a boat, next thing I know it will be a tank, you're a regular land, sea, and air *gonif.* You probably wanted this to happen."

"Look, I'm just trying to help you."

"Help yourself, keep kosher!"

"Here, give me your left hand," Ludwig said.

"I won't give you a hand, Mr. *Treyf,* but I'll give you something," he stammered and thrust his bloody hand towards Ludwig, an empty space where the index finger should have been.

If ever absence was presence, this was it – a terrible joke. Ludwig doubled over with laughter and lay on the ground.

"Grandpa, are you all right?"

"I'm fine, here, help me up."

As David helped him up, the paramedics put his night-flight companion on a stretcher and carried him towards an ambulance. Then the police came and asked everyone to leave the market until they could make sure that it would be safe to return. One of the policemen tried to speak to Ludwig, but when he realized that he didn't speak Hebrew, he turned to David and asked him a few questions.

"What did he want to know?"

"If we had any information?"

"What did you tell him?"

"That we just came to shop. He asked for our address and cell phone number and said they might want to speak to you in a few days."

"Not another interrogation," Ludwig said.

"What's that, Grandpa?"

"Nothing, really. Well, we've had enough excitement for one morning. We'll go looking for the scent and jeans in Katsrin tomorrow. In the meantime, let's pick up the car."

It was a relief to head up into the hills towards David's village.

"That was quite an adventure, Grandpa."

"Better than a disaster, David."

It was hard to believe, looking into the empty valley to his left and the unpopulated hills to his right, a few cows and horses grazing, that there could have been so much trouble only fifteen miles away and worse trouble, always a possibility, not that much further distant.

"I was worried back there, Grandpa, but I was proud of you, you didn't run away."

"Maybe I should have, I'm not sure he was worth risking my neck for."

"He's one of us, isn't he?"

"Unfortunately."

"What's wrong with him?"

"It's a long story, David, I'll tell you before I leave." This was the easiest thing to say.

"Look, Grandpa, God's hand again."

"I guess it always will be there."

"Yes," David said, "we'll always have this valley."

"David, I've been thinking, you have to go into the IDF in two years, why don't you come and live with me before you're called up? Once you're admitted to a college or university, you probably can get a deferment."

"But, Grandpa, I'm not sure they would let me do that. Besides, I can't leave my family and friends. You're family, of course, but you know what I mean."

"I worry."

"I know, Grandpa, but I can take care of myself. And sometimes you have to take risks, look at what you did today."

"Maybe it was a mistake."

"No, he's one of us."

"That's one of the problems."

"None of us are safe, Grandpa, unless he is, too."

"You've been reading too much Maimonides."

"I've learned a lot from you, too. Remember when you protected the Arab-Israeli who was being pushed around by some teenagers on the beach a few summers ago. You told me that sometimes you have to fight for what you believe in."

"I'm still worried."

"I worry about you when you fly to Israel."

"I was a little worried myself, the other night, I thought I might have been sitting next to a terrorist."

"Really?"

"Well, sort of."

"When can we go to Katsrin for the jeans and scent?"

"We'll go tomorrow and stop at Gamla on the way."

The next day, near the Daliyot Junction, Ludwig turned off the road at the sign for the Gamla Nature Reserve where hundreds of dolmens spotted the fields on both sides of the road. Long before the Roman siege of AD 67 by Legion X, nomads of the Golan had buried their tribal leaders beneath the basaltic megaliths.

According to Josephus in his *The Jewish War*, 4,000 Jews were killed in battle and another 5,000 met questionable ends in the Jewish revolt, a Warsaw Ghetto uprising before Warsaw, a Masada before Masada. Only two women survived – a slaughter house before the death-camps.

It was impossible not to reflect on a long history at Gamla. The Jews had lived with some success over varying periods of time in a number of nations and Empires – Moorish, Ottoman, Austro-Hungarian – but it never had worked out in the end.

If it wasn't the expulsion from England in the thirteenth century, it was the Inquisition in Spain in the fifteenth with Columbus, maybe a *landsman*, having the *sachel* to light out for the territory ahead. One way or other, they had hit the road before something hit them, like the butt of a Cossack's rifle. Like his own grandfather, like every New York Jew's grandfather, or so all the grandchildren of that generation had been told.

Not necessarily subjected to annihilation or eradication, torture or extermination, Jewish anxiety, in advance of disaster, for the fortunate, had been to move on to what seemed a safer place. For a hundred years, 1850-1950, it has been

mainly America, every Jew's promised land during that period except those few who, listening to Herzl, looked to
Palestine. Israel had changed everything, of course, especially now for Ludwig who was on a see-saw between two
worlds; and his balance wasn't always very good.

"What are those huts, Grandpa?"

"Dolmen."

"What's that?"

"I read somewhere that it's from an old French dialect and
means 'giant's table,' but archeologists think they were
tombs for small-time kings. There were too many kings in
those days for any one of them to be very important."

"If you're interested in tombs, we can visit Rambam's in
Tiberias one of these days."

"Rambam?"

"You know, Moses Maimonides. People come from all
over the world to see it."

"Only if we can have some baba rum after."

"Grandpa!"

"That's me."

"I know."

They sat on a bench on a trail overlooking the pyramid-
shaped hill that was sunk in the valley below so that its crest
was far below them. Griffon vultures and a variety of eagles
and hawks circled and settled on the cliffs of the ridges on
either side of the valley.

"Are you sure you don't want to come to live with me and
go to college in America? You can always come back and
go into the army later."

"I know how you feel, Grandpa, but this is where I belong. I'll always love America, you know that, but this is my
country now, and I have to stay with my friends. Some of us
will be in the same unit, even girls."

"That's nice, but it isn't summer camp, David, like the one I went to a million years ago in Kent, Connecticut, it doesn't take much for a war to start here, remember the summer of 2006?"

"I remember, you were the only one swimming in the beach at Ginosar, you said Hezbollah wasn't aiming at you."

"I was foolish, besides I was here. I could have been hit anywhere."

"But you stayed, Grandpa, you could have left."

"Well, I was here already, I couldn't run away."

"I can't run away either, Grandpa, that's something else you taught me."

"Maybe it wasn't a good lesson."

"Why isn't Gamla as well-known as Masada, Grandpa, the Jews fought to save their homeland here, too, and thousands died?"

"It wasn't unearthed and discovered until 1967 when Israel overran the Golan. It might take another war to keep it, that's what I worry about."

"You worry too much, Grandpa, you have to live in the now."

"That was always one of my problems."

"How long will you stay, Grandpa?"

"I'm not sure."

"And when will you come back after you leave?"

"Not sure about that either."

An Egyptian vulture, with its distinct black and white plumage, settled on a ridge only a few hundred yards away from them. There were many things he wanted to say to David now. Somehow, this seemed the time and place to say it, but he didn't want to burden the boy, there was still a touch of the boy about him, with the burden of his grandfather's feelings.

He might derive some strength from these feelings, but they also might prey upon him when he needed only to think about himself and his comrades, his and their safety in a time, if it came, of armed conflict and war. He didn't want David to be thinking about him when the boy was in a dangerous place.

A second of alertness might be the difference between survival and injury, or worse. This had to be his burden, not the boy's. He couldn't tell David he had feared for his life from the moment his mother had decided to make a new life in Israel.

This had been his secret and one that he might best be able to keep if he kept his distance, if he saw little of them during the next few years. He could find excuses for not visiting. Travel expenses and age were the simplest explanation. They would understand because they couldn't afford to visit America as a family. They knew he wasn't rich and hadn't found Ponce de Leon's Fountain of Youth, even though he had visited Florida fifty times and had had drinks at the Fontainebleau.

But he had to say something, and now might be the time.

"David, I have to say something. Now is one of those *now* moments."

"What is it, Grandpa?"

"You probably know this, but we'll always be together. You'll always be with me, and I'll always be with you, even when I'm gone."

"Grandpa!"

"We've got to face the truth, to be realistic, even on vacation sometimes."

"But why now?"

"I guess it's this place, what it tells us about the past and what it may say about the future. I can't quote Maimonides to you, but there's an American poet, Robert Frost, everyone has heard of him. I actually met him at college once. A lot of what he says gets quoted in those fancy Hallmark cards and their meaning gets lost, but then the meaning comes back somehow. He has a simple poem that I want you to read someday."

"What's it called?"

"The Tuft of Flowers."

"What does it say?"

"It may sound a little corny, but I want you to read it again one day when you're alone and in the right mood, when you're thinking about us and why I'm not by your side."

"What does it say, Grandpa?"

"Men work together," I told him from the heart, "whether they work together or apart."

"I see what you mean," David said, and he moved closer to his grandfather on the bench and put his arm around him.

"By the way, Grandpa, I have a job lined up for the summer."

"Great, what is it?"

"Polishing shofars."

"Sounds good, and it's better than polishing cars or waxing poetic if you don't have talent."

"Grandpa! By the way, thanks for the jeans and scent. I got Old Spice, yours."

He couldn't sleep well that night in his cottage on the kibbutz. Cottage wasn't quite the right word. It was a stucco-built holdover from the post-1948 War of Independence period with a moldering bomb shelter behind it. There was nothing charming about it, though there was something like a small quadrangle with flower beds in the center of the group of other houses, some of which now were occupied by Thai workers who worked the fields. But the view was good.

Sitting up in bed, with the curtains drawn open, he could see the hills beyond the Kinneret and the strings of lights along the ridges that he had become so fond of. They formed something like a circle and were satisfying to look at.

The hills were comforting to look at, but he still was wakeful. Sometimes the string of lights on the western side of the Galilee seemed to flash like the flare of a rocket, and sometimes they seemed to pulsate like tracer bullets. It was hard not to think of David, now a stretcher-bearer, being carried on a stretcher away from a battle zone.

No possible injury to the boy, however slight, was acceptable to him.

He didn't know what he would do in the future, but at dawn he would drive a few miles down the mountain road to the Offir Lookout, named in honor of a soldier who had died taking the Golan, and he would absorb as deeply as he could the calmness of the lake in this quiet hour, with a few small fishing boats out laying their nets, and think about all the good things that Marion's new life had made possible and the meaning it held for her and her family.

He would try to take mental photographs of all the good moments they had enjoyed together and store them for a future when he might need to look at them to convince himself that the risk she had taken to make a new life had been worth it, no matter what. Once he had taken these snapshots, he might want to keep his distance from them for a while. He might need these images, unaltered, to make life acceptable at some point in the future.

But he wouldn't tell any of this to Marion or David. The younger boys wouldn't understand in any case, and Gil, a *sabra*, who had been born into an acceptance of violence and war, wouldn't be able to understand Ludwig's apprehension. He might feel sorrow and despair someday about what might befall one of his children, but the grief would come *after* a loss.

Ludwig was a little less confused now than he had been a few days ago by what could happen in Israel and why it might happen, but he needed to protect himself. He wouldn't tell them that he was or wasn't coming back right away when he left this time. If they asked, he just would say that he always was with them and they always were with him, so it wasn't too important how often he came. They might accept this.

He fell asleep, perplexed, and in his dream he saw David, standing on top of Mount Arbel, an ancient shofar with a horn as large as an alto sax in one hand and a Tar-21 in the other. He reached to take the weapon out of the boy's hands, but the boy looked steadily at his grandfather and stepped back. He put down the shofar and the gun, looked over the lake, valleys, and surrounding hills, and seemed to say, *This is where I belong, Grandpa, this is where I have to stay.*

How had all of this come about? The boy and what he now stood for seemed to have come out of nowhere. How could his grandfather's floating, his ambivalences and ruminations, have led to this moment?

In his dream, Ludwig wept with pride, but knew he was dreaming and wasn't sure what he would feel or think when he awakened.

Chris Helvey's short stories have been published by numerous reviews and journals, including *Kudzu, The Chaffin Journal, Best New Writing, New Southerner, Modern Mountain Magazine, Bayou, Dos Passos Review,* and *Coal City Review.* He is the author of *Dancing On The Rim* and *Yard Man* (Wings ePress), *One More Round* (short story collection – Trajectory Press), *Snapshot* (novel – Livingston Press), *Whose Name I Did Not Know* (novel – Hopewell Publications), and *Claw Hammer* (short story collection – Hopewell Publications). Helvey currently serves as Editor in Chief of *Trajectory Journal.*

Photo by Nancy Parisi

Howard R. Wolf is Emeritus Professor and Senior Fellow in the Department of English (SUNY-Buffalo). A graduate of Amherst College (B.A.), Columbia University (M.A.), and The University of Michigan (Ph.D.), he wrote a psychological dissertation on Henry James. Twice a Fulbright Scholar (Turkey and South Africa), he has lectured as an Americanist, creative writer, and literary journalist in twenty countries. Widely published, he has pursued an interest in personality in memoir form (*Forgive the Father*), the novel (*Broadway Serenade*), drama (*Home at the End of the Day*), and short fiction. For the past fifteen years, he has created a character, "Ludwig Fried," in twenty stories who, living in the shadow of the Holocaust and various kinds of displacement, struggles still, often in comic terms, despite loss, to belong somewhere.
The Robert Frost Library, Amherst College, has an archive of Howard's lifework.

Made in United States
North Haven, CT
04 November 2021

10839814R00121